MANGOS & MISTLETOE

ADRIANA HERRERA

Mangos and Mistletoe
Written and published by Adriana Herrera
Cover by Cate Ashewood
Edited by Tessera Editorial
Copyright © by Adriana Herrera
Kindle Edition

ISBN: 9781710360059

This is a work of fiction. Names, businesses, places, events and incidents are either the products of the author's imagination or are used fictitiously. Any resemblance to actual persons living or dead, business establishments, events or locales is entirely coincidental.

DEDICATION

To all the Dominicanas scattered around the world finding ways to thrive.

ACKNOWLEDGMENTS

To the LatinxRom crew who in helped me grow this idea into a story. I am so grateful to have you all as part of my author family. To Annabeth Albert for helping me figure out this first venture in self-publishing. To my SC Sisters LaQuette and Harper Miller for all your support. And to Leigh Kramer and Nini for all your input about the story. I appreciate you all immensely.

Praise for Adriana Herrera

"Compulsively Readable."
-Publisher's Weekly

"Adriana Herrera writes romance with teeth—you'll laugh, you'll cry, and you'll be refreshed and inspired to fight even harder to create the vibrant, welcoming America in which her books are set."
—Suzanne Brockmann, New York Times bestselling Author

"Adriana Herrera writes family—all kinds of family—better than anyone else writing today"
—Cat Sebastian, bestselling author of "A Gentleman Never Keeps Score"

Mangos & Mistletoe

Kiskeya Burgos left the tropical beaches of the Dominican Republic with a lot to prove. As a pastry chef on the come up, when she arrives in Scotland, she has one goal in mind: win the Holiday Baking Challenge. Winning is her opportunity to prove to her family, her former boss, and most importantly herself, she can make it in the culinary world. Kiskeya will stop at nothing to win, that is, if she can keep her eyes on the prize and off her infuriating teammate's perfect lips.

Sully Morales, home cooking hustler, and self-proclaimed baking brujita lands in Scotland on a quest to find her purpose after spending years as her family's caregiver. But now, with her home life back on track, it's time for Sully to get reacquainted with her greatest love, baking. Winning the Holiday Baking Challenge is a no brainer if she can convince her grumpy AF baking partner that they make a great team both in and out of the kitchen before an unexpected betrayal ends their chance to attain culinary competition glory.

CHAPTER ONE

KISKEYA

Edinburgh, Scotland, Two Weeks Until Christmas Eve

"Third time better be a charm, carajo."

I repeated those words to myself for the hundredth time since waking up jetlagged and dangerously close to giddy this morning, in my Edin-freaking-burgh hotel room. After three years of trying, I'd finally gotten into the *Holiday Baking Challenge* competition, and this year the location was no other than one of my bucket-list countries—Scotland. I was literally living my best professional life in a place that was one of my *personal* life goals to visit, and now, I was running late.

I got into the elevator as I straightened my bomber jacket and looked down at myself, fretting about not being dressed appropriately. I'd gone for dapper, which was pretty much my version of dressing up. Blue Oxford shirt, under a heather gray sweater. Check. Slim fit Hunter green slacks and navy Oxford shoes. Check. This was as dressy as they were going to get me.

I was not into dresses, or skirts although…I did appreciate them.

Which was a good reminder for me to keep my eye on the prize. I was not here to thirst after Scottish women or to act a fool. I was here to work.

To win.

To take my career to the next level, and maybe secure my ability to stay in the States a little longer. I wasn't here to socialize. I wasn't here to make friends. I was here to land a job for the foreseeable future, and hopefully secure a work visa extension in the process. For the next week, I was Kiskeya Burgos, aspiring pastry chef and motherfucking machine, who lived and breathed to bake. Full stop.

Three years after leaving the Dominican Republic on my own, and hustling in LA kitchens hoping for a chance which could finally get me noticed, I'd made it. If I capitalized on this opportunity, doors would open for me. I could not fuck this up.

My focus and determination only lasted me as far as the front desk. Suddenly I was back to those first few months in the States when twenty-three-year-old Kiskeya—who'd never left the country by herself before—had to stop and take photos all the time because she couldn't believe she was really there.

The hotel was in the New Town of Edinburgh—which seemed pretty old as far as I could tell—and it was gorgeous. There were fireplaces everywhere and the decorations made everything festive. Lots of garland and even more tartan. It was lovely and warm and so different from what I'd grown up with in the Caribbean. It was almost a comfort to be in a place so different to home. I wouldn't have to think so much about what I was missing.

Before I could go further into my head, someone calling my name from across the room made me freeze mid-step.

"Ms. Burgos!" I turned to find Isla, one of the showrunners, rushing over to me as she tapped on an iPad. She'd been at the hotel when we'd arrived last night to welcome me and some of the other contestants arriving from the West Coast. But I'd been so out of it, I'd barely noticed what she looked like. She was cute—fair skin, jet-black hair in a messy bun.

From our brief interaction, I'd already liked her. She was friendly, but about her business, and I appreciated that.

"How did you sleep?" she asked, as she examined what looked like a very complex color-coordinated spreadsheet.

I nodded, trying not to geek out on her accent. Because I'd read my share of romances set in Scotland, and I was having a moment.

"I slept great, thanks. Too good," I confessed. "I'm late."

She popped her head up at that. "Don't fret. The first hour's for mingling. To give the contestants a chance to get to know one another." She waved a hand in the direction of a set of stairs. "Get some food and drink. Then we'll announce the teams and details for tomorrow." My back went up at the mention of the contest, and she grinned at what I was sure was a spooked expression. "Don't worry, the teams are going to be great." I must not have been hiding my skepticism, because this time she laughed. "Seriously, it's a great group this year. Once we've gone over everything, you'll all go on a city tour. You can see the city and spend more time together."

I perked up at that. It would be nice to get some sightseeing in. "Cool. I'm looking forward to it."

She smiled clearly trying to get me to relax. "We

arranged for a private tour at Edinburgh Castle, you'll do the high tea which is really posh."

I bit my tongue to keep from saying something super cheesy, because I'd been hoping for high tea.

Her iWatch beeped and she widened her eyes. "Ack, I have to go take care of something." She pointed at the marble staircase again.

"That's the room. I think everyone's there already. I'll come up soon. Go get some caffeine!"

I smiled at that and rushed up the stairs to the mezzanine, trying not to let my nerves get the best of me. I hated being the last one to arrive at an event. I never knew where to go. Who to say hi to first, where to sit. It took me straight back to the DR where everyone seemed to be gregarious and socially competent, and I could barely manage a family holiday without falling apart. People were hard to figure out. Baking. Kitchens. That's where I thrived, the language I understood. This type of situation usually ended with me putting my foot in my mouth.

Thankfully, as soon as I got up there, I was immediately greeted by a young woman who seemed to know where I needed to go. She glanced down at a grid of photos on the laminated sheet she was holding, then looked back up at me and stood to open the door. "Welcome, Ms. Burgos. Enjoy."

It wasn't a huge room, but it was decorated in the same festive style as the lobby. An easel to the side of the door held up a poster board which had the logo of the competition emblazoned on the top and read: *Welcome Holiday Baking Challenge Team.*

Just looking at that set off butterflies in my stomach again. This week was going to be a roller coaster. I did a quick scan of the room, hoping I'd spot someone from the airport van last night, and almost sagged with relief when I recognized one of the other West Coast contestants.

I made my way to him, grateful I wouldn't have to stand with my back pressed to a wall until I got up the courage to introduce myself to someone.

"Hey." Gustavo, one of the 'pros,' stood to give me a kiss on the cheek. He gestured to an Asian woman sitting with him. There were only four tables in the room, and they were all pretty close together. It seemed like we would be getting to know one another whether we wanted to or not. "This is Kaori. She's also from the Best Coast." He winked at his own joke, and I smiled.

I extended my hand to her, and she stood, waving me off. "I kiss hello too." She grinned as she leaned in to peck my cheek. "My ex was Cuban. After almost twenty years around his family, I don't know if I can even say hello anymore without kissing." Her smile was a little sad when we pulled apart, and I wondered what the story was there.

Gustavo was looking at Kaori like she was his favorite snack as he extended a hand toward her Vanna White style. "Kaori's one of the home bakers."

"It's great to meet you. I'm Kiskeya." *The Holiday Baking Challenge* was different than most baking shows in that they paired up a professional chef with a self-taught home cook. Each of us would be working with a stranger with completely different training than ours and counting on them to win the competition. I took a deep breath as I did whenever I thought about that terrifying detail and tried not to panic.

The thought of getting paired up with someone incompetent, or worse, someone perky and chatty—who thought I was there to make friends—had kept me up at night more than once over the last couple of weeks. But like I'd told myself a hundred times already, I would make it work.

I tuned back in to my fellow contestants, to find Kaori gesturing to the other table where there were four more people sitting. One, I recognized from the airport, but the others I had not seen before. "These are some of the others. Everyone, this is Kiskeya."

I sighed in gratitude at Kaori's assistance in introducing me. I went around the table shaking hands. The foursome included Alex and Derek. Derek worked as a pastry chef in a critically acclaimed farm-to-table restaurant in Asheville. He was tall, strapping, and *very* blond. He also had the seemingly required chef tattoo sleeves, complete with a man bun. When I first saw him in the hotel lobby last night, my judgmental ass had wondered if he was actually any good or if they'd picked him because he'd probably look great on camera. But I'd put Dr. Google to good use in my hotel room and the guy was no chump. He'd be a tough adversary, no matter who he got paired with. He was nice too, but that would not keep me from trying to beat him.

Alex stood when it was his turn to greet me. I couldn't help the smile that appeared on my lips when he approached.

"Are you a hugger?" he asked with his arms open wide. I wasn't usually, but he looked like a bear cub with glasses and I sort of needed some human contact. So I stepped in and was promptly wrapped into a warm hug.

As we pulled back, I tucked my hair behind my ear and smiled. "I'm not really a hugger, but I may be more open to them in the future. You're good at those." Everyone laughed, well everyone except for the two who I had yet to meet who were each doing something on their phones. I tried to not hate on them without at least knowing what their names were first, and focused on Derek, Alex, Kaori, and Gustavo, who actually seemed interested in getting to know me.

Derek smiled at Alex, and there was a glint in his eye that told me things were going to get interesting with those two. "Alex is also a self-taught baker, when he's not doing surgery on babies!" Derek's voice was full of awe and Alex's light brown skin reddened on his cheeks.

"I'm a pediatric surgeon in Atlanta." Alex smiled again, and I could already see why Derek was looking gobsmacked. They were almost complete opposites. Derek big and muscular, all in black. Alex short and stocky, with adorable blue-framed glasses and wearing a salmon-colored cashmere sweater. But there was definitely something there.

"I'm very happy to meet you, Alex, and very impressed with the fact that you find time to bake competitively. I hope you're on my team because surgeon hands are the kind of nimbleness I'm gonna need to beat all these people." The foursome laughed again, as if I wasn't 100 percent serious.

After a moment, Alex stretched a hand to the women who were still sitting and doing their best to ignore us. His smile was not nearly as warm when he spoke to them. "These are the Beccas." As soon as he mentioned them, their heads popped up, and I instantly got a strikingly similar pair of chilly smiles directed at me.

The first one, dark-haired and blue-eyed, with eyelashes that even I, with my remedial level makeup game, could tell were fake, extended her hand to me and winked. "I'm Rebeka. With a K." That brought on a giggle from the person next to Rebeka-with-a-K, who seemed oddly identical to her but for the bright auburn curls and brown eyes. She also regaled me with lots of teeth.

"I'm Rehbecca, with an R-E-H...no K." That last part was said in unison with the other Rebeka.

Extra. Very extra.

I said a silent prayer to the food competition goddess— as I took in their eerily similar outfits of very tight Gucci everything—that I didn't end up paired up with one of them.

I hoped this week wouldn't involve mixers and chats either because that would get old fast. "Nice to meet you both." I was going to ask who the home baker was when Gustavo spoke up again.

"Rebeka-with-a -K's a pretty big influencer on Instagram. She invented the hashtag"—he actually did air quotes —""Cupcake cuties.'"

I did recognize her. I also thought her shit always looked mad dry and mediocre for the amount of followers she had, and I was petty. "Oh no, I don't think I know that hashtag."

Rebeka-with-a -K twisted her mouth to the side at my reply. Later I'd probably have to think on why I was out here trying to make enemies—but these women were fucking snobby.

The other one went next. "I'm a pastry chef at Milk Mama's." Another LA fad bakery.

Be nice, Kiskeya.

Nod, smile. "I know Milk Mama's. Your, uh...Donut Cakes broke the internet." Because people had no damn taste. "Nice to meet you." Rehbecca, with an R-E-H was side-eyeing me hard, and I decided I was pretty much peopled out. But Rehbecca wasn't done.

"What do you do?" My chest tightened at the question. Heat spreading on my face as I opened my mouth to answer. It wasn't that I was embarrassed. I was proud of what I'd been able to do on my own. But it wasn't the goal

I'd set for myself when I left the Dominican Republic and decided to try my luck as a pastry chef. Still, I made a living, and I was slowly making a name for myself.

"I'm working in a few kitchens right now. Trying to get my own business off the ground. I do pop-ups. Mostly custom-made cakes and events. Burgess Fine Pastries." The name was my compromise at finding something that didn't erase me completely, but was neutral enough to not get pigeonholed into an "ethnic" bakery. Just one more of the lessons I'd learned in these three years.

"Oh, that's nice." I had to admire the degree of unimpressed derision Rebeka-with-a-K was able to inject into three words. But I didn't need to stick around for more of it.

I hiked a thumb over my shoulder. "I'm going to get some food."

The rest of the group went back to chatting, and as I walked by, Kaori pointed to the two empty seats on her table.

"Come back and sit with us. Sully's sitting here." She pointed at the empty chair next to her. And just as I was about to ask who that was, a hurricane of brown curls, tartan, and perfectly shaped burgundy lips barreled into the room.

Fuck me.

I reminded myself that I could not afford distractions—especially not the life-sized one headed my way. My only hope was that this person worked for the Edinburgh crew and would not be making the trip with us to Ayrshire Castle. I hadn't prayed since the day I got on the plane to leave Santo Domingo, but it was all I could do keep from crossing myself when I got a good look at her.

I pushed my fists into my bomber jacket, still not daring to sit at the table, or anywhere that would get me in close proximity to this embodiment of a sunbeam. And it wasn't just me, everyone in the room seemed to be bewitched by her smile. Even the Beccas looked up from their selfie-posting frenzy to watch her as she made her way across the room.

Was life in slow-motion now? It likely fucking was, and I seemed to be rooted to the spot, as the force of nature with curly hair glided over to us.

As discreetly as I could, I brought my gaze down to her feet and slowly made my way up. She was wearing brown ankle boots and hunter-green tights, the exact same color as mine. Her skirt—a knee-length thing in dark blue and green tartan—hugged every one of her curves. By the time I got to the denim shirt and leather jacket, I could feel the beads of sweat trickling down my back.

Breathe, Kiskeya. Tranquila.

She came to a dead stop right in front of me and didn't even try to hide she was checking me out. My skin prickled as dark brown eyes, like the darkest chocolate, smiled at me.

"I'm Sully." Her hand was warm and soft. Her nails trimmed to a sensible length but painted in the same burgundy matte shade as her lips.

I opened my mouth and was impressed with my ability to make words. "I'm Kiskeya. Nice to meet you."

Her smile got even wider, if that was possible, and the big gold hoops on her ears bopped against the mess of curls which cascaded down her neck and shoulders, as she shook her head.

Her lips were perfect. And kissable, so fucking kissable. "Kiskeya."

Holy shit, the way she said my name.

I literally stumbled back. Hand on my chest, eyes scanning the room looking for the spot where the thunder had come from. Because surely this throbbing in my head could not be her. And then she spoke again, in perfect Spanish.

"La tierra de mis amores."

Oh God. She knew what my name meant.

Before I nodded woodenly and hopefully said something that didn't make me sound like a complete and utter dolt, I had one last fleeting thought.

Kiskeya Burgos, your distraction is Dominican.

CHAPTER TWO

SULLY

A tall drink of café con leche, with more café than leche—just like I took mine.

And her name was Kiskeya.

Yes. Por. Favor.

My gaydar could not be beat, and the woman with the Dominican name who looked like my every fantasy was staring at me like she wanted to gobble me up, her eyes darting from my face down to my boobs. She also seemed to be on the verge of passing out, so I let go of her hand and decided against the kiss on the cheek. I was fresh, but I wasn't trying to violate anyone's personal space, and Kiskeya looked spooked.

But I was me, so I had to say something. "I assume you're Dominican, because even the most devoted fans of the DR's beaches aren't gonna go as hard as naming their kid the Taino name for the island." I was clearly joking, but she just seemed to get even more pressed. I was a lot and was used to having some kind of effect on people, but scared shitless usually wasn't it.

"I'm Dominican. Came to the States after college." She

closed her eyes at that and shook her head as if reconsidering. "I came for culinary school like three years ago and stayed."

Okay, she came after college, but had no accent at all. She had to be on the West Coast too, because all the East Coast peeps were on the same flight from New York. There was a story there for sure.

Sully Morales, you are not going to get all up on this woman's business.

But man, I wanted to ask a million questions, starting with what soap she used because I was getting verbena and ginger and those were two of my favorite things. Thankfully Alex saved my thirsty ass from myself.

"We have two Dominicanas in the house. Fun is all but guaranteed." Kiskeya did not seem to like that, but she kept her stank face in check. I figured she didn't want the attention on her, so I starting messing with Alex.

"I'm here to compete to the death, Alex. Your cute behind should be thinking about how you're gonna beat me," I teased as I sank my butt into the seat, then realized I needed to go and get some food. Kiskeya was still standing by Kaori's chair looking like she was debating between running away or hiding under a table. I wasn't going to leave my fellow Dominicana hanging, so I popped back up and tried really hard to offer a genuine smile.

"You want to go and grab some food? I think Isla and the rest of the crew will be here any minute to tell us the teams and instructions for tomorrow."

Flinching was not the reaction I was hoping for, and Kiskeya sounded unsure even when she answered, "Okay."

I was kind of thrown. Meeting another Dominican anywhere usually meant lots of laughter and inside jokes, but so far, Kiskeya seemed to want to get as far from me as possible. She kept looking around as if figuring out where the nearest exit was. Or maybe she just didn't want to talk to me. Maybe she was staying on task. We were most likely going to be on opposite teams, maybe she didn't want to get friendly. It was disconcerting, and that extra side of me wanted to prod a bit. Figure out why she was acting all put-out.

By the time we got to the buffet, she hadn't said a word.

"So, what would you do with the prize money if you won?" I asked, genuinely curious. She seemed so serious, I assumed she had it all figured out.

She looked at me for a second and went back to examining the offerings on the buffet. When she spoke, it was low, as if she didn't want anyone else to hear. "Honestly, the money isn't my biggest priority. Although I can definitely use it, but the reason why I entered the contest was the paid apprenticeship at *Farine et Sucré.*"

"Ah, that makes sense, if you're on the West Coast." One of the prizes for the "professionals" in the contest were their choice of paid apprenticeships under some of the most renowned pastry chefs in the country. I knew one was in New York City with a Mexican female chef who owned, Canela, a very popular bakery in Brooklyn. Seemed like Kiskeya wanted the job with the French dude in LA.

"It's basically impossible to get in there, but everyone that's apprenticed there ends up getting snapped up by the biggest kitchens. It's my dream job." I guess the way to get Kiskeya fired up was to ask her about business.

"That's a big motivation to give this your all." I was trying to be encouraging, now that she was at least talking.

She nodded, as she inspected a cheese plate. "More than my all. I will do whatever it takes to get that job."

And I would very much avoid thinking about why I was

bummed out when I realized Kiskeya wasn't interested in the East Coast job. *Sully, you met the woman get three minutes ago. Get over yourself.*

This was also a great time to remind myself that I was here to focus on me. Not to get tangled up and in my feelings about someone who I'd never see again once this contest was over. This was what I did. Found something or someone to focus on, so I didn't have to figure out my own shit.

"How about you?" I yelped when Kiskeya spoke, because apparently I was going to be a full-on weirdo today.

But when I processed what she'd said, I froze at the question. It had been a long ass time since anyone had asked me what I wanted. "I kind of got volunteered for this."

She literally did a double take and just stared, like she could not compute what I'd just said. "I didn't enter myself. My family entered me."

More confused staring.

"I mean, they asked me before they did. They thought it would be fun, and honestly I never thought I'd get in."

"Oh, okay." Her tone clearly conveyed, "I don't know how to respond to that," and she immediately went back to a deep analysis of the grilled tomatoes and mushrooms in one of the chafing dishes.

I was kind of annoyed at her lack of interest in me, but then I reminded myself that what people thought about me was not something I wasted my time on. I could only control what *I* chose to do. And I was determined to keep it nice and breezy while I was on this free vacay in Scotland.

We went through the buffet line slowly. Kiskeya examining everything closely as if she was trying to figure out how they made it.

"Spread's amazing." I really could not keep my mouth

shut. She turned to look at me, like she'd forgotten I was there, and again, I felt my annoyance bubble up. Why was this chick getting to me like this?

"Yeah, it's a pretty nice brunch menu...I've—"

"Ooh, they have morcilla." Because I had no manners, I interrupted her, but this was my favorite.

She seemed surprised at my excitement. "You like morcilla?"

"Of course I do."

She grabbed the tongs after I'd taken a couple of pieces of the black pudding and put some on her plate. I just put whatever on my plate as I closely tracked her every move, intrigued by this quiet Dominican woman, who didn't seem interested in me in the slightest. Eventually she turned to look at me, and my face heated, realizing I'd been standing there staring. But instead of calling me out, she went in another direction. I followed her, because today I seemed to have developed an appetite for people ignoring me.

"Morcilla isn't something all Dominicans like." Uh, okay, so what did that mean? That I gave off a "Basic Dominican Bitch" vibe?

I didn't pout, but damn, it was close. "My abuela made it for us every year when we came to visit. Like homemade."

Oh, now I was getting glares, this b—

"Homemade morcilla *is* the best. Depends on the cook, of course." This would've been a great moment to bail on this tragedy of a conversation, but did my ass stop rambling and leave her alone? No. I talked all the way back to the table.

"My parents are from Bonao, so we'd go back every summer to visit the family. We always went to see my grandmother for a couple of weeks."

We put down our plates, sat, settled bright red linen

napkins on our laps, and grabbed our cutlery, but still no response from Kiskeya. I felt my heartbeat in my throat and my face was hot from her indifference. I'd been ignored before, of course, but I usually knew who to expect it from. My mother always said I'd never make it as a poker player, because I showed everything I was feeling on my face.

So I kept mine away from Kiskeya. If she didn't want to talk to me, I wouldn't talk to her. Kaori and Gustavo had headed to the buffet again, so I couldn't turn my attention to them. I focused on my food instead. As I was cutting into a poached egg and mentally calculating how long it would take me to eat my food—so I could use my empty plate as an excuse to get the hell away from this rude-ass lady—she finally spoke. Her voice startled me so much, I dropped my knife and the clatter it made sounded like a gunshot had gone off in the room.

"I was born in the capital. I lived there until I moved to the States." Despite my commitment to being rude to her, I immediately turned my face in her direction, still interested. "My parents are from the south. But we never really went there growing up."

Her eyes looked so sad, and of course my dumb heart wanted to immediately make it better. I wanted to ask questions, figure out why talking about home brought about such sadness in those gorgeous brown eyes. I wondered if she was close to her family. I knew Dominican families could be a lot; zero boundaries and the toxic masculinity in our culture could wear women the fuck out.

Still, I couldn't imagine my life without my loud and loving mother and little brother. Even after the last couple of years when I'd had to put my entire life on hold to take care of my mother, I still didn't regret a thing. But before I could say any of that, Gustavo and Kaori got back to the table. And just as they were sitting, we saw Isla come in with the competition's hostess.

Alex grinned and wiggled his shoulders excitedly as we watched them walk up to the front of the room. "This is it, guys." His eyes actually sparkled, and when I turned to Kiskeya, I noticed that her face was taking on a yellow pallor.

I wanted to reach for her hand and squeeze. Tell her not to be so nervous. That we could support each other while we were here, because my self-preservation instincts were seemingly at an all-time low. But instead of reassuring her, I went with pettiness, because I was also a mess. "Don't worry, what are the chances they'll put the two Dominicans together?"

She frowned, probably not sure how to react, and I opened my mouth—almost certainly about to make things worse. Blessedly I was saved from myself by Isla's voice.

"Good afternoon, team. This is your official welcome to the Holiday Baking Challenge week." There was a round of applause, and the energy in the room definitely shifted. "You've been selected among some of the best up-and-coming young pastry chefs and home bakers in America. Feel proud of yourselves for that." More applause and even some whoops from Gustavo and Alex, which had us all laughing.

"We have some information to share with you today, but I will leave all that in the hands of the show's leading lady." She extended her hand to the Puerto Rican comedian-turned-baking-show-hostess who'd been the face of the competition for the past two years. Patricia Calderon looked as amazing in person as she was on television. She was wearing jeans, a thick sweater, and tall, brown leather boots

—makeup and hair on point. She smiled at us with genuine excitement.

"Y'all got your food, taking advantage of that bottomless boozy brunch," she said with a snap of her fingers. "Get your mimosas, people. The Cooking Channel's paying!"

That elicited a laugh from the room, and I took that as a cue to take a sip, because I was all kinds of jittery. Between the glances Kiskeya kept sending my way and the anticipation of who I'd end up paired with, I was feeling the nerves.

For some reason, I'd convinced myself there was no way they'd pair up Kiskeya and me. That would be such cliché, putting the two Dominicans together as if we would be kindred spirits. Like that hadn't been my exact thought the moment I'd realized she was from the DR too. I could be a little cliché and I was definitely sentimental—Kiskeya didn't seem to be either. She would probably not be thrilled by the prospect of being stuck with me for six days. The applause brought me back to what was happening in the room, and I realized the announcements had begun.

"I know you've all gotten brought up to speed on the program." A flurry of affirmative responses were heard across the room at Patricia's statement. She flashed perfectly straight teeth at us before going back to reading her notes. Everyone was hanging on her every word. Even the Beccas had put their phones down for a moment.

"You will have three days of challenges with a practice day in between." The space hummed, with every new nugget of information raising the excitement levels. I noticed that Kiskeya had pulled out a tiny pad and pen from somewhere and was dutifully taking notes. Of course, her nerdery just made her that much hotter to me. I was hopeless.

Patricia went on giving us the rundown of the themes

this year. First challenge: holiday cookies, then bread, and the third day would be a surprise for the first day of filming. Kiskeya frowned adorably at that, squinting at her paper like she could coax an answer from it.

I leaned in and whispered in a low voice, "I might have to copy from your homework later." She practically jumped in her seat, and suddenly all I wanted was to lure Kiskeya to me like a wary kitten. There was not much about the woman that was soft, and she certainly didn't seem like she was interested at all in getting anywhere near me. But still, the pull to unravel her a bit, to see what was hiding behind all that sternness was very strong.

"She's about to tell us who the teams are." I even found her hissing sexy. Obviously, this was not a Kiskeya problem, this was a Sully problem.

I tuned back in to Patricia's voice since Kiskeya had shifted in her seat, so that she had her full back to me.

She was not subtle...but I knew I hadn't imagined the way she was looking at me when I walked in. There had been something there, but I wasn't going to get pushy either.

"As you all know, we're very mindful of how we pair our teams." She was clearly trying to reassure us they were not going to do us dirty, but you could still cut the tension with a knife. "We put together pairs who can join forces and bake interesting and delicious treats for us, and this year we have a bounty of talent." That got some smiles and laughs because there was nothing more smug than a cook getting compliments. "Our first team is our Southern power pair, Alex Smith and Derek Barstad. We're so excited to see how Alex's soulful flavors fuse with Derek's Scandinavian creations."

"I'm still gonna beat you boys!" I was a clown, and the

tension did ease a bit after that. And both Alex and Derek looked very pleased with the outcome.

The next team was Kaori and Gustavo, who both seemed happy and even I had to admit his Central American-inspired bakes with Kaori's Japanese delicacies sounded like a fascinating combination.

Kiskeya was leaning in so much that she was almost doubled over as Patricia got ready to announce the last two teams. I surprised myself when my heart started beating so fast I could feel it all the way up my throat. I was nervous. Because as much as I'd told my family I didn't care if I won the competition, that I just wanted a chance to prove to myself I could do it—I really wanted to win. I wanted the money. To finally have the resources to do something for myself, so who I got paired up with mattered. And honestly, the Beccas scared the shit out of me. When I glanced at Kiskeya, I saw her look between the Beccas and our table with worry. I wondered if she was trying to decide what was worst.

"The third team," I heard Patricia's voice through the fog of my own fretting, "was sort of a no-brainer, because we want those ratings and we could not pass up a chance to advertise a team called the Beccas."

Fuck.

I glanced over at the two women in question, trying hard to avoid the horror that was surely making an appearance on my teammate's face. They looked smug, and I promised myself I would do whatever it took to beat their asses. I held myself tight, my chin up, as I stared straight ahead at Patricia and waited for her to actually say it. Dreading what Kiskeya's reaction would be, hoping she wouldn't say something that would make me feel small.

"And last but not least, we have our Dominican Divas!"

People applauded, and with every word, I felt like another bolt was tightened on my neck. "We have the home baker bringing all the Caribbean flavors and the pastry chef who's determined to earn the chance to work at one of the world's most renowned pâtisseries." I did turn then and saw the blood drain almost completely from Kiskeya's face. She looked like she wanted to be anywhere but here.

With a knot in my stomach which felt like it would choke me, I leaned in again, knowing I would almost surely make matters worse.

"Don't look so spooked, mija. I promise I don't bite." My teammate's back somehow got even straighter, and because I had no fucking sense, I opened my mouth again, this time so close I could smell her shampoo. "Unless you ask, of course."

That did not get me a smile. At some point I'd have to ask myself why hearing Kiskeya Burgos say my name pronounced in pissed-off Dominican Spanish, set off a flurry of butterflies in my stomach.

CHAPTER THREE

KISKEYA

"Everything's fine... E-ve-ry-thing's *fine*."

That was the mantra I'd been repeating from the moment I heard who I'd been teamed up with. I mean, what kind of messed up cliché was this?

Putting the two Dominicans together? What the hell? Because that's all it was. They wanted us in a team, so we could put some adobo in the show or some shit.

Well, they were in for a hell of a surprise. I was not some Dominican spice fairy. I was a cranky bitch with a job to do. If they needed comic relief, I was not the motherfucking one.

I slumped on the seat of the luxury van that was taking us from our hotel up to Edinburgh Castle. Because now that they'd paired us off, we were supposed to be "building rapport." It was going to be a hell of a week. I was dreading how things would go with Sully; we were already butting heads. Mostly because I was being a grump. But once I started, it was hard to turn it off, and she seemed to get off on teasing me. Also her general hotness made me nauseous in a way that could only end poorly.

I kept my head down, but let my eyeballs drift to the seat next to mine where the baker in question was looking relaxed, chatting with Alex and Derek who were in the row in front of us.

"I'm so excited for the Christmas high tea!" She squealed in excitement, and I felt the sound somewhere between my ribs and other places that would remain unnamed. "Isla said we'll have the tea room all to ourselves." Another squeal, and this time she must've pulled a face too because Alex's booming laugh sounded through the van.

"I've always wanted to come to Scotland. It's wild this is how I ended up being able to come. I've been reading up on the area where our castle is!" She sounded so thrilled. Fuck, why did she have to be so pure? "We're right by where they filmed *Outlander*."

"*Outlander*! Oh my goodness, there's no chance we'll run into Jaime, is there?" Kaori's fangirl moment managed to even pull a laugh out of me.

"What are you excited about, Kiskeya?" I guess I could not make myself invisible after all.

When I looked up, I found matching expectant looks from Kaori, Gustavo, Derek, and Alex. The Beccas opted out from the tour, saying they were going to bond by doing a little shopping, because a basic bitch will be a basic bitch. But my row companion was offering no more encouraging stares—what I got was withering side-eye and a new version of unbothered.

I wanted to say that I'd been wishing for a trip to Scotland for years too. That this was a dream come true, but instead, I went with the most asshole-ish version of me I could conjure up. "I wish they'd just let us start practicing. It seems sort of wasteful not to use the time to get ready for the contest."

The eyeroll Sully directed my way told me everything I needed to know about how my comment landed with her, and the rest of the teams exchanged various iterations of "What's her problem?" looks.

"Kiskeya, you need to chill."

If a person could speak in side-eye, Sully would be fluent. And apparently, unlike the rest of the bus who seemed to understand I wasn't in the mood for cheer, she got right back into my space.

"You want to go to the Christmas Village tonight?"

I was going to have to start carrying an extra stick of deodorant in my pack this week, because being around Sully had my perspiration levels at an all-time high.

Also, was she immune to stank face?

"Umm no. I don't think I'll be going the Christmas Village." I knew I could be scary when I was pissed. My face could make grown men tear up, but Sully was currently nodding along as I shot her down and tapping on her phone.

"They have a North Pole house." How were her eyes so big, and her eyelashes legit almost touched her eyebrows. I wish I could look away. I did my best to give off hardcore grumpy vibes as we stepped off the van, but she was relentless. "It has a bar!"

Alex perked up as soon as he heard the reference to alcohol. "Where?!"

"There's a Christmas Village North Pole bar." Why was I enunciating?

Sully nodded as we all followed the driver who would hand us off to the tour guide. "Yes, it should be fun. Kiskeya and I are going tonight. You guys want to come?"

Wait, *what*?

I opened my mouth about to protest, when Sully let out

a high-pitched squeal and turned in a circle. "Oh my God, this view is amazing. Guys!" she yelled at the others, one hand waving them to her and using the other to tap on her phone screen. "We're in Edinburgh; we're together." She threw her head back, looking up at the sky. "It's a moment." She said the last word with such reverence, like she could hardly believe she was really here. It made us all stop in our tracks.

When I looked at her with her hair down now, honey-colored curls flying in the afternoon breeze, her face golden from the setting sun, I knew I'd have to work very hard not to get carried away by this girl. I was feeling her so much, I had to get some distance.

I hung back as the others gathered on either side of Sully, her arms stretched high looking for the best angle. I told myself the pit in my stomach was absolutely not want, because I wasn't doing that. I was here about my business, and my business was not Sully Morales.

"Kiskeya, ven." My whole body thrummed when I heard her call my name. I turned my face to where they were standing, my thick heavy hair whipping in the wind. Even with strands all over my face, I managed to spot her.

Ven. Come to me, she said. And as if her hand held a string to my core, when she crooked her finger, I did.

"Here," Sully said, as she placed an arm around my shoulder. "Scoot down a little and tip your head up." She clicked her tongue at whatever she saw on the screen of her phone, making the others laugh. "Come on, Kiske, smile like you're on top of a mountain about to tour a castle, chula." The glee in her voice made my lips turn up despite myself. Her arm tightened around my shoulder and impossibly, I smiled wider.

"Don't call me chula, Sully." Even to my own ears, I

sounded a lot more delighted than annoyed. The truth was, even my surly ass couldn't help getting caught in the moment.

I heard a kissing noise from behind my head, and my stomach dipped like I was on a roller coaster. "Okay, no more chula, mi chulita."

I just shook my head, too nauseous to respond.

After the selfie photoshoot—it took multiple tries before Sully deemed we had a photo worthy of the Gram—we were greeted by a docent who showed us around the castle. Giving us all the inside gossip about what the past dwellers of the massive building had gotten up to. Between Sully, Alex, and Gustavo's silly questions and opinions on pretty much everything, it was hard not to feel the excitement of the day.

By the time we walked out of the castle and were back in the bus headed to the hotel, it was dark. The high tea with prosecco made me malleable enough to let Sully catch me in a moment of weakness.

She was riffling through the bag of trinkets she'd bought at the castle's gift shop when she asked, "You're coming with me the to the Santa bar, right? Team building, Kiskeya. It's team building." She informed me, waving a hand between us.

It was just light enough outside for me to catch the smile hiding behind her mass of curls. Oh my stupid, stupid heart. I wanted. I wanted so much, my chest tightened and my skin prickled. That light-headedness that was usually the precursor to bad, career-ending decisions tried to edge out all the rules I'd set for myself on the way here.

Rule number one: No distractions.

"I don't know if the Baking Challenge's idea of building rapport is getting drunk with a bunch of fake elves."

Why did her laugh make me think of flowers? Stupidly, I thought, she should always be wearing a crown of them on her head.

"I didn't say we needed to get drunk with the elves, just walk around. We're going to be stuck in that castle for a whole week."

I tried to tell myself, one night out wouldn't hurt. A few drinks with my teammate would be a good way to get to know each other, but I knew better.

Rule number two: No ill-advised crushes.

"I'm almost one hundred percent sure the Beccas ditched us to go find a commercial kitchen somewhere to practice, Sully. I can't blow this."

It was as if all the anxiety that I'd managed to keep down all afternoon flooded back into my head at once, and suddenly, I was short of breath. There was too much riding on this. I closed my eyes, thinking over what I'd just said. Trying to untangle what was real from what was worming into my head.

"Hey." I opened one eye and found Sully's concerned brown eyes on me. "Forget about the Beccas. We got this." Her hand rubbed circles between my shoulder blades, and slowly, I felt my breathing even out. Despite my reluctance to come on the tour, Isla and Patricia had been right. It had been good to hang out with everyone. But the way I was responding to Sully...there was danger here for me.

I kept my eyes closed when I answered Sully, I didn't want to look at her face as she realized she'd gotten stuck with a hot mess. "I'm not going to take a bunch of selfies with fake elves, Sully. I have a couple hundred Instagram followers and a reputation to uphold."

"Did you hear that, Kaori?" she called to the front of the bus where Kaori and Gustavo had been sitting with their heads close together, probably scheming how to beat us all. "My partner has a whole two hundred followers on Insta. I got myself an influencer, bitches!"

That had everyone laughing again and me helplessly shaking my head, which seemed to be my permanent state with Sully. It was safer than getting distracted by her mouth, and I needed to set a hard line of not looking anywhere south of her collarbone. Every minute, *every second* with Sully seemed to flip a switch inside, lighting me up as she went. Keeping my head in the game was basically survival at this point.

"You guys better get yourselves together because we've got the Dominican Dream Team over here." She bumped my shoulder, and I finally opened my eyes, and came face to face with all that was Sully Morales. "We're going to blow them away when we hit them with Tropical Storm Sullkis."

I would not survive this contest if she kept looking at me like that.

"Did you just mash up our names?" Helplessly, I started laughing at her ridiculousness. I could not remember when I'd felt this excited and terrified at the same time. Probably since before I left the island.

"I sure did. Team Sullkis is about to take this challenge!" She yelled with her head thrown back, obviously trying to rile up the others.

"Oh, so your name's first?"

"Duh. Of course my name's first. I made it up! Also KiSull doesn't roll off the tongue. Team Sullkis is *it*." This was said with finger snapping and shoulder shimmying. "They won't know what to do when we hit them with the DR flavors. We're going to work magic with some mangos and coconuts. Bring the tropics to Scotland."

She bit the tip of her tongue, sharp teeth letting me only

29

get a peek of pink. And I swallowed hard. This girl. She made feel too much. Getting carried away, letting my feelings interfere with my professional life, mixing business with pleasure was a mistake I could not afford.

Rule number three: No kissing your kitchen partners.

I turned my head away from her before I said it, "I need a little space, Sully. You're just a lot. I get that you want to 'do it for the culture' and everything." I felt like an asshole making air quotes. "But I'm not going to be all over-the-top Dominican. That's not my style."

As soon as I said it, I felt terrible, but maybe if she hated my guts, then I could focus on this contest. The "what the fuck" from Sully that followed my words got drowned out by the driver informing us we'd arrived back at the hotel.

We stepped out of the van in silence as I waited for the cussing out that never happened.

"I'm not up to going to the Christmas Village after all," she said as she walked out of the bus, not even bothering to look at me. "But this isn't the end of it, Kiskeya. You're not the only one in charge here."

She walked toward the revolving glass door leading into our hotel, but she stopped right before stepping in, her head only half-turned when she spoke to me. "I'm not going to start some drama, so people can talk shit about the Latinas getting into it before we even started, but if you really want space, you're going to get it. From now on, it's all business."

CHAPTER FOUR

SULLY

Fuck Team Sullkis.

What the hell was "over-the-top Dominican" anyways? I knew she had to be serious since Kiskeya was too fucking stuck-up to even attempt humor, but that shit last night had been totally uncalled for. Especially since we actually had fun at the castle together. Sure, she'd started off grumpy, but by the end she was chatting and all smiles. And I lost count of the times I caught her looking my way like she was trying to drill a hole through my bra. Kiskeya wasn't fooling anyone with her "I am an island" mess.

I'd been ignoring her all morning and had opted to sit at the back of the van that was taking us to the castle where the competition would take place. It was hard to stay really mad while driving through the Scottish countryside though, because man, this place was pretty.

I took a photo of a particularly lovely stretch and sent it to my mom and brother, to go with the few others I'd taken. It was a little early for them to see them, but they'd be texting as soon as they woke up. I'd been checking on my mom more than necessary. It was the first time I'd been away since she'd gotten hurt, and I was feeling overprotective.

She was fine now, was even doing the books for the family bodega again. I'd promised my mother I'd be selfish this week and I was trying. I'd even been hoping I could take selfish to the next level and get some high quality making-out in this week, but Kiskeya was pissing me off.

My phone buzzed with a text, distracting me from seething about my teammate's bullshit.

Hey mija. I love it. It's so green over there! Are you feeling better? I'm sure you can work it out. What are the chances you'd end up with another Dominicana? That's a sign, baby. You're going to win this thing.

I sent her a short message asking how she was feeling and thankful this fancy bus had Wi-Fi, so I could at least take my mind off the massive fight that would surely go down between me and Kiskeya later. There was no fucking way, *no way*, I was going to cave on incorporating the DR's flavors in our bakes.

Nuh-uh. We were going to fight. I was *not* coming all the way to Scotland to bake a bunch of bland shit because Kiskeya had a complex. She needed to work that shit out in therapy like the rest of us did. If I wanted to get my mango and piña on, I was going to do it.

"Wow. Sweetheart, that is *not* a friendly expression." It was hard to stay pissed when Alex was around. He was like a pint-sized, extremely well-groomed brown teddy bear, but even he couldn't get me out of my Kiskeya-induced funk.

"I'm not feeling friendly," I grumbled, as I moved over to give him room to sit by me.

"Here," he said, passing me a cup with something warm in it. "It's spiked hot chocolate. The driver has a thermos." He cupped his hand over his mouth. "I'm going to see if I can convince Derek to take advantage of me later."

I snorted at his goofy expression and gingerly took a sip of the very boozy sweet drink, then craned my neck to see what the rest of the bus was up to.

"With the way he was looking at your mouth when you were eating those strawberries this morning, I'm thinking he'd be more than happy to." I could only spot Derek's messy blond man bun and resisted the urge to stand so I could see what "Ms. I Need Space and I Hate the Tropics" was up to. "You seriously won the teammate lottery. You got a hot Viking who can bake, and I've got a moody Dominican who hates me."

That last part was said in a full huff, complete with my arms crossed tightly against my chest.

"Okay." Alex stretched the word for a full half minute as he assessed me from under long dark lashes. He came closer, and when he spoke, it was barely above a whisper. "So things aren't going well. What happened? You guys were getting along so great at the castle. But the energy was definitely off by the time we got to the hotel."

"What had had happened was—"

Alex sucked his teeth and brought his hand up and down a few times, clearly concerned that my volume would give away our gossiping.

"Sorry." I cringed as various pairs of eyes landed on us. "Anyway, things *were* good. We were messing around about how we were going to beat..." I casually pointed my chin in the direction of the Beccas. "And then I said we'd do it with our Caribbean flavors, and she shut down." Now I was the one speaking barely over a whisper. "She went all stiff and told me I was a lot, and she needed space, and that 'over-the-top Dominican' isn't her style." I made the air quotes, feeling heated once again about how ridiculous she was being.

Alex's face at least gave me some validation, because yes, this shit was really fucking weird. "Maybe she's really introverted and needs her alone time?"

Of course I'd thought about that, and the space thing hurt a little, but it wasn't the issue. I didn't expect to be besties with her. "If she needed space, she could just let me know that. I'm not a toddler," I complained, trying really hard not to sound like one. "But the whole thing about me being too Dominican...that's going to be a problem. I'm not going to downplay my culture for anyone." Just thinking about Kiskeya's foolery got me mad all over again. I wouldn't say it to Alex, because I was already oversharing about our disagreement to a competitor, but what hurt was that I really thought us having the same roots would bring us together.

He had turned around to presumably look over to where Kiskeya was sitting and gave her a considering look. "Do you think she meant it as a way to maybe not create expectations that you'll *only* use tropical flavors?"

I pulled a face, and he immediately shook his head. "Maybe she wants to stand out by doing something unexpected, like maybe *not* using Caribbean ingredients."

I knew I had to be staring at him like he'd lost his mind.

"I don't mean *at all*. I just mean—"

After a moment he closed his eyes and shook his head again. "You know what, forget what I said. I don't get it."

I cracked a smile at that and bumped his shoulder. "I like you, Alex. Too bad I'm gonna have to whoop your ass. I'll let you hold the trophy, though." We both cracked up at that, and after a minute of admiring the landscape, we went back to our spiked hot chocolate.

Alex's sight was trained on Kiskeya again, and he seemed as confused as I was by her. "I mean it's not like you're all in your face with the Dominican. Sure, you mention it a lot, but it's cute."

"Alex, don't make me pinch you," I threatened, pressing my thumb and index finger.

He giggled, like I wasn't serious, and said in a low voice, "Maybe she just wants a Dominican Lite kind of vibe."

I was about to say something along the lines of "Tough luck, bitch!" when an idea started forming in my head.

"Oh no, girl. That eyebrow's 'deviousness is afoot' high. What are you scheming?"

I smiled at Alex's wary expression and then looked at my nails. "I like you, boo, but I still want to win, so Imma keep this to myself."

"Okay, babe, I'm going to go check on the blond bombshell; gotta keep that team spirit high."

"Uh-huh." I watched him walk back to the front as my idea started hatching. Kiskeya thought I was extra...I was going to bring the Dominican up to a fifteen. By the time I was done doing the most, she'd think a few bakes with some mango and guava were a fucking breeze.

CHAPTER FIVE

KISKEYA

"Where did you even get plantain chips? And I guess we're talking again? I didn't mean you had to stay away from me, Sully. I just need space, that's all."

I needed to dial it back with the tone because this was the first time since yesterday my teammate had even acknowledged my existence.

"Yes, we're talking again," she said, chomping on a chip. "It's not like I have a choice. We're stuck together, and I'm not letting you overrule me on what we're baking, Kiskeya."

Crunch. Crunch. Glare.

"Seriously, where did you get chips?" I had no idea why I was so fixated with the bag of fried plantains, but I was practically vibrating from needing to know. I didn't even like plantains—one more way in which I was a defective Dominican—but the smell was making me salivate.

It had to be the jetlag.

I waited for her answer as I tried not to stare too hard at the neckline of Sully's gray sweater dress. It showed just a tiny peek of her cleavage, and the edge of something lacy and burgundy (again) which was making me perspire. A lot.

"I brought them with me. I got a bunch of them in my suitcase."

There was a little black bow right at the base of her bra strap, and I wondered if it would come off if I tugged on it with my teeth. A finger snap by my ear made me jump.

"What?"

"For someone that asked for space, you're certainly getting very up close and personal with my chest area." She was wearing a nude shade of lipstick today, and when she pursed her mouth...it was hard to focus. "Eyes up here, Kiskeya."

Fuck. Okay, that was the look of someone who knew exactly what her boobs could do to a person.

I swallowed twice and tried very hard not to let my eyes drift below her shoulder. "You brought them from home?"

"Yes, I did, because I didn't think I'd find them here and they're my favorite snack." That last part was clearly meant to make a point. I hadn't expected her to handle anything I said yesterday well, but I panicked.

There was just too much happening all at once. Sully's entire vibe had me totally off-kilter. In one afternoon, she'd almost made me forget all the rules I'd set for myself. I knew what could happen when people got carried away with a colleague. How messy things could become. I'd seen it a million times. A kitchen is a place where discipline, focus, and respect for the craft made all the difference.

I'd seen my fair share of affairs gone sour, bad judgment turning into harassment. Egos destroying careers and partnerships. Sully had never worked in a professional kitchen; she didn't know how toxic it could get. So if it took her thinking I was a stuck-up bitch to get her to keep her distance, then that's how it would have to be.

Still, we had to work together. I put a hand up in

concession. "Look, Sully. I just like to keep things strictly business. And the whole 'Dominican pride' stuff...It's not my thing."

"Not your thing." She stared at me like I'd grown a horn, while my throat went bone dry. Just as Sully was about to tell me whatever was on her mind, the van came to stop, and the oohs and aahs from the rest of the passengers derailed us from having it out in front of the other competitors.

"Oh my God. I can't believe we get to stay here for a week." The awe in Kaori's voice made us both turn.

A gasp from Sully felt like the perfect reaction. We were here, all of us. This bus full of people from all walks of life. We'd all gotten here by what we could do with our hands, our skills in the kitchen. I shuddered out a breath thinking just how far I'd made it from that day three years ago when I'd gotten on a plane in Santo Domingo. All the missteps. All the times I thought I'd have to give up. That I just could not cut it as a chef, or worse, that my parents were right and I'd made the biggest mistake of my life by leaving home.

Maybe all of it happened so I could end up at this moment.

"It looks like something from a movie." I didn't know who said that, but it did. There was still green on the ground and the blue sky was only pierced by the gray stone of the castle. There was a circular driveway right in front, but beyond that, there was a lot of green with the occasional patch of snow. Sully squeezed my shoulder, and I took that as a truce.

"Let's go, everyone. It's time to get settled in. Practice starts in two hours." Isla's announcement got me moving, but when I tried to stand, Sully's hand stayed on my shoulder.

"We need to figure something out, Kiskeya. We're never getting a do-over with this."

I nodded and followed her out of the van and into the castle.

I felt like I was messing everything up with Sully, that with every word, I was making things worse. I asked for space when what I wanted was the opposite of that. I offended her by saying I thought she was too much, when the reality was I couldn't get enough.

I was ruining everything, and no matter what my reasons, antagonizing her was not smart.

"Kiskeya." I snapped out of the tornado of thoughts roiling around my head and realized I'd walked into the castle and was standing in the foyer already. I inhaled deeply and let out a slow breath.

"Hey." Sully's voice was so much kinder than I deserved. "The concierge is about to take us to our rooms. Are you all right?"

Not even close. "Sure, thanks." I did something with my lips and teeth that I hoped looked like a smile, and turned my attention to the guy wearing actual livery who seemed to be working double time on his tablet.

"Damn, he's gonna poke a hole in that thing." Derek was not the only one concerned about the tablet. Even the Beccas were cringing at how hard he was tapping on it.

Isla bypassed him—probably not wanting to get caught in the crossfire when he put his finger through the glass—and attempted to command our attention again.

"Okay, teams. You will be shown to your rooms by Leith. Each pair has to share a suite." There weren't protests immediately, but she put up calm-the-bear hands anyway. "But we've made sure everyone has their own bed—"

Leith put a hand up and started shaking his head so hard, Isla stopped talking. When he leaned to whisper in her ear, I knew some bullshit was about to ensue.

"Oh no." The dread in Sully's voice echoed exactly what was going through my head.

"Yeah, my man's looking real pressed." Gustavo was shaking his head in anticipation of whatever bomb was about to be dropped.

"I freaking knew it," I hissed to no one in particular. "Castles look nice, but they're old. Watch them tell us we're sleeping in trundle beds."

Isla's face went from surprise, to annoyance, to resignation in five seconds flat, and I braced for it.

"Looks like there's been a slight change of plans."

"Shit, she's showing way too many teeth for this to be anything but terrible news." When even Sully started getting antsy, I had to say my cell number backwards, just to keep my anxiety at bay.

Isla cleared her throat as the protests started—I noticed mostly from the Beccas. "The production company had requested two beds for all the suites, but it looks like the only room with two beds is on the ground floor. Kaori and Gustavo have that one."

No. No. *No.*

"I need my own bed. I'm a very light sleeper." That was Rebeka-with-a-K who I'd seen sleep through an entire round of charades on the bus this morning.

I really wanted to protest too, because being in one bed with Sully was almost guaranteed to turn into a disaster. But if I said anything now, after all the stuff I'd already said to her, I knew she'd take it personally and the tiny window I still had to work on her not despising me would close forever. Kaori had also mentioned she could not do stairs, and I wasn't going to be an asshole about her getting the only room which could accommodate her. So, I kept my mouth shut and worked on minimizing the screaming in my head.

Isla cut her eyes at Rehbecca with an R-E-H and then turned to the rest of the group. "Folks, I'm very sorry. But it's too late for anything to be done today. We need to go over the details for day one, so we don't run behind schedule." She pointed at some part of the castle beyond where we were all standing. "You have to check-in about wardrobe. If some of you really do need a bed, we can definitely try and bring some by tomorrow."

"Fuck."

I cringed at how put-off Sully's tone was. It sounded like she really didn't want to be in the same room with me, and I didn't blame her.

Isla kept trying to text and tap on her tablet as she figured details out, and after a minute, she perked up. "Wait. Looks like the cottage in the property is big enough for all three judges. So we have another room with two beds. How are we deciding who gets it?" She raised a shoulder and looked at Leith who seemed to be completely out of his depth with all these Americans in his castle. "We could draw straws!"

"Um...we're good with just one bed." Sully's snort at Alex's very enthusiastic tone made a laugh bubble up from my chest despite the tension in the room.

Derek was looking a little too smug for those two not to be up to something. That meant the two-bed room left would be decided between us and the Beccas, and they looked bloodthirsty. I caught a glimpse of Sully who was standing, straight-shouldered, clearly trying not to look in my direction.

It smarted because I'd done that. I'd made her stiff and weary when she'd been nothing but bright and sunny to me. I had to fix this. I needed to show her my weirdness had nothing to do with her. I had to be the one to offer the olive branch. Before I had a chance to talk myself out of it, I opened my mouth, hand up in the air. "Actually, the Beccas can take the room. Sully and I should be okay, right?" I only sounded slightly hysterical when I pivoted my head in my partner's direction.

She was not feeling me though, and gave me a very long and unfriendly look. "Suuuuuuure." She sounded anything but—still Isla jumped on that in a second.

"Perfect! Thank you so much, Sully and Kiskeya, for being flexible." She gave the Beccas a withering look, but those two only had one setting, entitled. "This time, Leith will really show you to your rooms. There are packets for each of you with all the information you need for day one." She smiled knowingly at the way everyone picked up their pace. All of us eager to find out what was in store for us.

"Once you read through your binders, the teams with 'first shift' practice should be here in one hour. The others need to report to wardrobe and makeup. Welcome to the Holiday Baking Challenge Week everyone!"

We all shuffled up the stairs, and Sully and I were the last ones making our way to the rooms. When the rest of the group was out of earshot, she came to the dead stop at the landing and turned a very cold eyeball in my direction. "All of a sudden you're not in need of space. Or fed up with my Dominicanness."

I was proud of myself for not covering my face with my hands, because I was sure I was turning red, despite my highly melanated complexion. "I never said I was fed up with you."

I kind of had, and we both knew it. Oh...she looked really devious when she raised her eyebrow like that. God, her mouth was really close to mine.

"What if I like sleeping naked?"

Breathe, Kiskeya.

"It's too cold." I actually gulped, like in old-school cartoons.

Oh, that husky, throaty laugh. That sound could turn my core liquid. I could just melt away. "Sully," I gasped, not even sure what the hell was happening.

"Kiskeya." My name on her lips, Kee-keh-iah. It was like being home, like sinking into the water at my favorite beach. Lukewarm and crystal clear. Where everything made sense. It had been over three years since I'd felt that kind of comfort, nothing had even come close. I let out a shaky breath, barely daring to move a muscle, frozen under her stare.

Her hair was brushing the side of my face now. I closed my eyes and gripped the banister as I waited, for what I wasn't sure. It was hard to think with Sully's coconut and lemon smell seemingly everywhere. I leaned in and her lips brushed the curve of my ear. My nipples tightened, just from that light contact. Fuck, I was in so much trouble.

"I always run hot, Kiskeya. You should've realized that by now."

I swayed a bit and watched her walk up the hall—my heart slamming against my chest like a rubber ball—hoping like hell I hadn't just played myself right out of this contest.

CHAPTER SIX

SULLY

"That is a very big bed." I grinned at the groan coming from somewhere behind me as I made my way to the gigantic four-poster bed. I'd realized that Kiskeya Burgos was kind of precious. I'd never seen so much red on brown skin. Baby girl could blush. And I kind of liked pushing her buttons.

I made a show of bouncing on the mattress, then lay back on it, arms stretched out. "This will do."

"Sully, be serious. We need to read our packets." I could hear she was flustered even if she was trying very hard to sound annoyed. But seeing her pressed was kind of fun, so I patted the spot on the bed next to me. "Bring them here."

She looked kind of cute when she was pissed. "Sully, deja eso. It's a big box, you need to come here." She was waving her hands at the two packages that were sitting side by side on one of the desks in the room.

"Okay, I'm coming. So testy."

I smiled when I got there and noticed her box was still intact. "Awww, roomie! Were you waiting for me to open them?"

She shrugged, looking adorably embarrassed. And as I'd noticed she did whenever she was a little bit outside of her depth, she took the ever-present elastic band on her wrist and did her hair up in a tall ponytail. Putting her perfect cheekbones and big brown eyes on full display.

She never wore any makeup. Just a little bit of lip balm. But otherwise, her face was always fresh. I'd caught myself staring at those perfectly shaped lips more than once. Kiskeya was beautiful. Like "wreck my life" gorgeous, but there was a sadness just under the surface that made me want to make all kinds of bad choices.

"You ready?"

Right, the boxes. "I am."

We tore into them like kids on Christmas morning. My box had a red apron with my name stitched along the top, and I saw Kiskeya pull out chef whites with piping the same color as my apron. Her name was stitched on hers too.

She ran a finger over the letters, and there was just a slight tremor in her hand. Her reaction made my own chest tighten. This was big, and it felt imperative to do something to mark the occasion. I jumped, remembering I'd brought some pins to put on my apron.

"Wait!"

She looked up from admiring her chef whites, her brows furrowed. "What?"

"I have something for you." Right when I was about to show her, I realized she might not want what I was about to give her at all. "Actually, never mind." I waved a hand in dismissal of the idea and went back to my apron.

She huffed in apparent frustration. "Come on, Sully. What is it?"

I felt dumb now and wished I hadn't said anything. I had the suspicion I was just going to get a rebuff, and the little bit of goodwill we'd managed to create between us would go up in flames.

"It's nothing. Forget it."

Kiskeya's eye rolls were pretty epic, but I was too jittery too smile.

"Dejame ver." This was going to be my kryptonite, when she got all stern in Spanish.

"Fine," I said and fished them out of my backpack. "Here." I thrust my open palm toward her.

She furrowed her brow and picked up the little heart which was one half Dominican flag and the other half the Pride one.

"You can use that one. I'll use my brujita pin," I explained, as she examined the heart a bit more.

When she finally looked at mine, she laughed. "Is that a witch in an apron?"

"No," I protested. "It's a brujita with an apron. Put your pin on your whites Kiskeya. The DR flag is not gonna give you cooties."

She flattened her mouth at my accusation, and I immediately felt bad. I always walked around telling people not to make assumptions about others, and here I was doing it. I just wanted to know what was going through her head. Why she looked at me with such longing in one moment, and could be so closed off the next.

Kiskeya looked down at the pin on her palm, then fisted it as she worked out whatever she was going to say. I was beginning to regret starting this, but I also knew myself, and if we didn't have this out now, it would be worse in the long run.

Finally she looked up, but didn't make eye contact when she spoke. "Sully, it's not that I don't love my country. I do, but it's complicated, okay?"

She turned her gaze and finally met my eyes for whatever came next. "I really don't want to sound like an asshole, but I don't know any other way to say this." She cringed, as if already anticipating how I'd take whatever she was about to tell me. "The DR is not an ancestral home I went to for a few weeks in the summer. It's where I lived my whole life, you know? And even though I love it, I also know I had to leave it. I couldn't be my full self there, not really. I haven't been gone long enough to romanticize some of the stuff that was hard."

Fuck, I really misjudged this. "I hadn't thought about it that way."

To her credit, she didn't scoff or roll her eyes. "I'm just trying to live, Sully. I don't hate myself or my roots, but I've also been cut down more than once for 'bastardizing the classics' when I've tried to do something like back home, or put my own spin on a recipe. I don't want to be humiliated. So yeah, I'm careful of not overdoing it in the kitchen. It's shitty that I have to think that way, but it is what it is."

I had no idea what to say, so I went with what I was feeling. "Can we start over?"

She smiled, and I was sure it was the first real one I'd seen, because it practically obliterated me. If I thought Kiskeya was beautiful before, soft and smiling Kiskeya was devastating.

She thrust the hand without the pin toward me. "Me llamo Kiskeya, y soy Dominicana."

I gripped her fingers in mine and pushed up to kiss her on the cheek. "Soy Sully, y soy Dominicana tambien."

We stayed like that for a few seconds, our fingers intertwined, and then she put the pin on her whites. She did so carefully, and when she was done, held it up in front of her, her eyes solemn. "Thank you."

I nodded, feeling the moment a bit too much. "This is a big deal for you." With every word I got Kiskeya a little bit more. And in the process I could feel her getting all the way under my skin.

She pursed her lips, brown eyes piercing me. "Isn't it for you?"

Of course it was, but I didn't want to give it power over me. "I want to do well. I'd love to win." *But if I don't, I'll be fine.* I didn't say it because we both knew it was not the same for her.

Something passed over her face, but I couldn't tell what. "We need to start getting ready. We have to read all this before practice." And just like that, she was back to business.

She pulled out a binder from the box, then tipped her chin toward mine. "I think we each have one of these," she offered, as she flipped pages.

I dug out my binder, a twin to hers, and brought it to the loveseat right off the fireplace in our room. As chill as I wanted to be about this, with every line I read, the excitement built. Kiskeya sunk into an armchair right across from me and started reading out loud.

"Three challenges. All in one day." She didn't need to state the obvious—it was going be a grind.

I nodded, reading my sheet. "First one is a classic with a twist."

She picked up where I stopped. "They tell us what to make, but we can do whatever we want with the flavors. They picked rugelach and Linzer cookies."

"Nice. What do you want to do for the twist?" I paused from reading up on the time we'd get for the challenges and competition rules—since I knew I'd brought our first potential argument to the forefront, but Kiskeya was ready for me.

She held up a hand pleadingly. "Can we read through and then talk details? Please?"

I sighed, "I heard what you said. I get that you've had bad experiences before, but for this competition, we have no reason to hold back on everything." I needed her to get that I wasn't going to let her steamroll me on this. "We need to meet halfway."

"I'll try." She was fighting dirty with that pout. I lifted a finger and pointed in the direction of the lips in question.

"I need to keep my eye on you."

Oh, a shy smile. Be still my motherfucking heart.

"Second challenge is called 'When in Scotland'!" She was really fucking cute when she was excited.

"Yeah, looks like we'll be doing an elaborate version of a traditional Scottish recipe."

She looked up from the binder, beaming. "Shortbread Houses."

There wasn't any information for the third challenge which we knew was the Showoff Showcase. That one was the same every season, only the theme changed. All we got was how long the challenge was and a clue.

"Ornaments?"

I nodded as I recited the rest of the instructions. "Yep. Seems like each team will get three hours of practice today. We're lucky we're on the second shift. We get more planning time."

Kiskeya scowled as she read, her teeth gnawing on her bottom lip. "We have to go see the makeup people." She made a face, and stuck her tongue out at the binder, which had me cracking up. "I don't like makeup."

"You'll be fine. Just let her know you like a natural look. Also, I'm not sure what wardrobe means. I'm wearing leggings and Nikes."

Kiske dipped her head in agreement. "Same."

"Looks like that's all the info we're getting for now," I proclaimed as I slammed shut my binder, needing to get my mind off Kiskeya's ass encased in spandex. "We have a little bit of time before we have to go down. What challenge do we fight about first?"

Kiskeya brought her wrist up to look at her iWatch then eyed me with just a hint of something that looked very fucking close to flirtatious.

Oh shit. Where was this coming from? And why was she leaning in so close?

I felt like prey with the way she was looking at me.

"I fight dirty, Sully."

I wanted to ask what else she did dirty, but instead I just licked my suddenly very dry lips, as Kiskeya looked poised to pounce.

"Is it hot in here? Do we need to open a window?" I sounded flustered and that elicited a wicked laugh from my baking partner.

"Feeling warm, Ms. Morales?" She smiled but made sure she kept her distance. "You'll cool off now. I just wanted to show you that you're not the only one who can make people sweat."

I had to laugh at how smug she looked. "Turnabout's a bitch, I guess. Me asusta, pero me gusta."

She threw her head back at the reference to an old ranchera song. "I'm not sure what the biggest lie is: that you'd be scared of me or that you like me."

I was surprised to feel a lump in my throat from hearing her say that. "I like you."

She lifted a shoulder. "I'm not the easiest person to deal with. I'm too intense and sort of snobby."

Okay, yeah, these were true statements, but that didn't

50

stop me from wanting to make her feel better even though only hours ago we were barely speaking. "That doesn't mean you're not likable."

She smiled, but it was so sad, like she knew eventually I'd change my mind. I wanted to fix all of it. To tell her I'd already realized I'd been wrong about her, but before I could think of how to say it, I felt the pad of her finger on my temple. "You had some glitter from the box near your eye."

She ran her thumb over the spot a couple of times, and I felt a pool of heat gather between my legs. I wondered what would happen if I turned my face just an inch so her wrist was right against my lips. If I darted the tip of my tongue out just...for a second.

Her breath caught as I looked up, and she held my gaze, her hand still on my face.

What were we supposed to be doing anyway?

Fuck. She *was* fighting dirty and this was *such* a bad idea. We hadn't even started the contest and I was already muddying the waters, and I was going to keep wading in too. I turned my head just enough to catch her palm with my teeth. I bit gently into the soft skin, and my pulse thrummed. I could feel the rush of blood to my head.

Kiss me.

Just. Fucking. Kiss. Me.

Once again I caved first and leaned forward, but after a second, she leaned too. I could smell the lemongrass, sweat and her own scent. It was all intoxicating. This kiss would probably ruin this whole week, and I didn't care. I closed my eyes when her warm breath touched my skin.

"Time for wardrobe check!"

The pounding on our door almost gave me a cardiac episode, and by the time I figured out what had happened,

Kiskeya had pulled off some kind of ninja move. She was all the way on the other side of the room opening the door, and telling whoever was there we'd be down in a minute. I just sat on the couch gasping for breath.

She closed the door and leaned against it, looking as winded as I was. "That wasn't smart."

I opened my mouth to say something, but before I could get a word out, she grabbed her shoes, tucked them under her arm, and escaped.

CHAPTER SEVEN

SULLY

We'd had a busy couple of hours, and now were in the kitchen ready to get on with our practice time. Kiskeya took the almost-kiss in stride and had been all business as we made our way through makeup and wardrobe, afternoon meetings and finally to the studio kitchen.

We were wearing aprons we'd found hanging on hooks by our workstation. The brand-new red ones were reserved for filming tomorrow, and I was leaning against a counter, observing Kiskeya as she sat on one of the enormous butcher tables. She dangled her legs as she read through the new packet we'd gotten from Isla. She looked so young. She was only twenty-six I'd found out during lunch after Kaori had asked. Two years younger than me, but she'd been all on her own for three years now.

How was I going to resist kissing her? Whenever she blew a stray strand of hair off her forehead, the need to touch her practically gnawed at me. I glanced at the gray fitted sweats and cream-colored Sherpa hoodie she was wearing today. She kept it simple, with clothes, hair, everything. She had that mix of butch and femme that got me every fucking time. Her limbs long and rangy. There was power in that body though. It was hard to focus with her so close. I knew it was more lust than anything else, but all I could think of was running my hands over all that bronzed skin.

"Sully!"

Fuck, I'd been staring.

"Sorry, was just thinking of recipes."

She gave me a sideways look which told me she knew exactly what I'd been up to, but she was too excited with whatever she'd just read to give it much thought. "Did you read the judges list?!"

I hadn't; they always had the same two and a rotating guest. I honestly didn't care who it was. Apparently that was not the case for Kiskeya, who was more animated than I'd seen her so far. She jumped down from her perch on the table and came to stand next to me, stretching a hand to flip through my notebook until she found what she wanted.

"See! Jean-Georges is the visiting judge!" I knew this was supposed to be big news for me, but I was drawing a complete blank. Kiskeya let out a frustrated sound and threw her hands up in the air.

God, how could I want to fuck someone this bad and find them so adorable at the same time?

"He's the owner of *Farine et Sucre!*" Oh right, the Dream Job. "We have to be on our A game, Sully. I really want to impress him."

This was how I kept my hands and my lust to myself. By remembering that Kiskeya was here to get a job at a pâtis- serie in LA—across the country from where I lived. Hell, I had an out. Six days and we'd each go on our way. Full stop. Easy, breezy, no complications.

"I got your back." And whatever that twinge was somewhere in my chest when I said it, well, I was just going to ignore it.

"Thanks for saying that, but we really do need to start figuring out what we're going to make. I don't like feeling unprepared, and believe me, it's not pretty when I do."

She pulled open the binder and went to the notes section. There were pens and pencils on top of the desk, and I got up to grab one for her.

I knew this conversation was going to have its bumps, but now that we were on the verge of starting to work as a team, I couldn't help feeling that frisson of excitement. Kiskeya would be a great teammate; she would give it her all. And that would push me to do the same.

"Let's do this! Team Sullkis is about to bring the platano power to Scotland."

She shook her head in response to my comment then wrote something on a blank sheet of paper. "I'm thinking for the Linzer cookies we can do a sugar plum flavor."

I twisted my mouth to the side, unimpressed. "What the fuck is a sugar plum?"

That eye roll was going to get old real quick. "It's not a real fruit."

Okay, Dr. Obvious. "Duh, that's why I asked what the hell you were talking about."

Her scowl was also not my favorite, but I wasn't going to start fighting first. I kept quiet while she elaborated on the sugar plum idea. "We can poach the plums in mulling spices, maybe with a little ginger, then make a jam."

That did sound kind of good, but I had an idea too. "How about guava? Linzers are a shortbread type crust and guava would work great. Don't glare at me, Kiskeya Burgos."

All right, a stare-off then.

She didn't say anything for a full thirty seconds, and I

knew she was trying to figure out how to shoot down my idea without pissing me off.

"Your face is going to get stuck like that." I was a brat. So the fuck what?

To her credit, she went with probably the most soothing voice she could manage. "Guava's fine, but it's kind of predictable. They're going to expect us to come with something super tropical out of the gate. Why not go for something more whimsical, Christmassy?"

"Guava's Christmassy." Oh yeah, that eye roll was going to be a problem.

"It's not in Scotland, Sully. At least admit the sugar plum idea's good. We can infuse the butter with Earl Grey for the crust. It'll be aromatic and a nice match for the jam."

"Fine."

I really wished I didn't find her smile so damn hot.

"I have an idea for the rugelach too."

"Of course you do." I had my arms crossed tight against my chest, genuinely pissed now. Because clearly Kiskeya's idea of teamwork was actually the Kiskeya Show.

"Hear me out first. How about hot chocolate rugelach?"

Dammit that idea was really good too.

She smiled very mischievously, and I knew my non-poker face had foiled me again. "Admit it. You like my idea."

"Perhaps." I wasn't going to throw her a party.

"We can put a little cayenne in it, make it like a Mexican hot chocolate."

Now, it was my turn at an eye roll. "That's not Dominican."

"I know, but it's got a hint of Latinx flavors. We can do a marshmallow nougat, crush it up, and roll it into the chocolate spread."

I waited to answer. I wasn't going to gush over her shit—

not when she was hogging all the recipes. "I'll let you have this challenge," I held a finger up in the air for effect, "*If* I get to pick how we do the shortbread houses."

I could hear her jaw creaking from where I was standing.

"Kiskeya, I'm not going to go along with whatever you decide for every challenge. We're a team. I got here just like you did because I can bake like a boss. You're not the only one with skills."

At least she looked embarrassed. "You're right." She shoved her hands into her hoodie pocket. "What are you thinking for the houses?"

I let out a breath, trying to relax, and smiled thinking of the ceramic casitas that my mom collected over the years on visits to the DR. She had them all displayed in a cabinet in our living room. "How about making some casitas?"

"That just means *little houses*." Damn, she really was looking to set me off.

"Yo hablo español, Kiskeya. I meant the traditional houses, with the pastel colors and the white woodwork. They have them all over the Caribbean and Key West."

She thought about it for a while and then nodded. "But that's not festive."

"I could pipe little string lights, maybe do a little church with the steeple and garland in front." That seemed to hit home.

"That could work. And it's tropical, but not like we're trying to hit people over the head with the Dominican."

Again with this. "We're going to have to find a middle ground, Kiskeya."

From one breath to the next, it was like she put a wall up. "We can do the pastel houses. That's fine. Do you have any ideas for flavors? We need to start working on this."

I sighed, throwing my hands up. I thought we'd gotten somewhere earlier, but we seemed to be back to square one. "Lemon and coconut. Valencia orange and clove? Maybe nutmeg?" She nodded with her back turned to me, as she started pulling things from the enormous pantry.

"Sounds good. Let's get started."

Oh, it was like that? Well, I wasn't fucking ready, and I was about to take the Dominican to an eleven.

I went to my tote bag and pulled out the palo santo wrapped with white sage I'd brought with me, but decided not to use since Ms. Thing was so damn touchy. But I was all tied up in knots, and I needed some of this bad energy to get cleared out, or this bake was going to be a disaster.

I turned on one of the ranges and lit it. I moved around the kitchen as Kiskeya tried her best to ignore me, and just when I was about to come around a second time, she let out a full scream. "What the hell are you doing?"

"What does it look like I'm doing? I'm saging the kitchen."

Her eyes got bigger with every word. "Are you trying to fuck with me, Sully?"

"Kiskeya, everything I do is not a personal affront to you. I do this whenever I'm in a new kitchen. It's just something that helps me get in a good headspace; this has nothing to do with you."

She pushed herself off the counter she was leaning against and ran a frustrated hand into her hair, doing and undoing her ponytail like three times.

"This is not going to work if you keep pushing me like this." She was tugging hard on her hair, and I could see that she was legitimately distressed.

"Kiskeya, what is really going on? This," I said, holding up the barely burnt sage. "Can't be what's got you like that.

I get you have complicated feelings and all, but I can't be on pins and needles about everything."

"I'm not doing heart to hearts. I'm sorry if I gave you the impression that I'm here to make friends. I'm here to win. You do your part, and I will do mine. And in five days, hopefully we each walk away with half the prize. That's it."

I gulped down the dumb tears that were trying to push up my throat and walked to the sink to put out the sage. It almost didn't make sense. I could tell she'd been trying not to piss me off. But as soon as there was any chance we'd overdo it with the culture, all bets were off.

It was so far from my own experience. Growing up, my culture—knowing that no matter how much I was made to feel like the other outside, at home I had an identity no one could take away from me—had always been lifeline. For Kiskeya, it seemed to be the opposite. I was annoyed at her for being so stubborn, at myself for letting all this get to me... at whoever had made her feel this way. But for now, she was right. We were here to win this contest, and whatever was going on with Kiskeya was not anything I could fix. So, I tightened my apron and went to set up without looking at her again.

"Let's get started, then."

CHAPTER EIGHT

KISKEYA

"Breathe, Kiskeya." Sully's voice was so low that I almost wondered if I'd said it to myself.

I let out a long breath and looked down at her. She was tired. I could see it in the set of her shoulders, but she'd been a machine today. She was a few inches shorter than my five-nine, but she was a powerhouse in the kitchen. Amateur or not, Sully was a skilled baker, and I was lucky to have her as a teammate.

The rugelach and Linzer cookies had come out well enough, but we hadn't wowed the judges. The clear winners of that first round had been Kaori and Gustavo who'd gone all-in with Central American and Japanese flavors. Their black sesame rugelach and hibiscus and yuzu marmalade Linzer cookies had the judges literally swooning. I had to bite my tongue when Sully looked at me and said in an angry whisper, "I told you." She didn't need to say about what.

Now, we were waiting to be judged for the second challenge, and I was wrung out. I looked at the other teams standing in pairs at the end of their stations, waiting for the judges to come and look at the shortbread houses. I wondered if their hands were shaking as hard as mine were.

There was no way to anticipate the intensity of this day. Kitchens were always high-adrenaline spaces. The best ones run like loud, well-oiled machines where everyone and everything has a place to be and a job to do. But this day had been like nothing else I'd experienced. I felt out of my depth so many times, forgot how to do things I'd done a million times. And through all of it, Sully held it down, calmly getting me back on track. But there'd been no warmth. Not since last night.

"You ready?" Sully asked with urgency, as the judges approached Alex and Derek who were on the station before ours.

"I am. You?" A sharp nod was her only response.

I straightened my whites and looked at the beautiful casitas Sully had piped with such care. They were perfect little replicas of the houses my family had driven through whenever we left the city in the DR. Being with Sully these past few days had me thinking more about home than I had in years. Although the usual pang that came with those memories didn't seem as strong. There was just too much to process when it came to Sully and the effect she had on me, but none of that could happen right now.

"What do we have here?" My back straightened as the three judges and Patricia approached us. They stood on the other side of our work station inspecting our display.

Sully side-eyed me, chin pointing at the judges, but I shook my head. She should be the one to explain what we'd done. It had all been her idea. Her face went from annoyance to confusion. Probably wondering why I wasn't rushing to kiss up to the judges, but she recovered and soon was launching into an explanation.

"These are our key lime coconut casitas." She looked up at me, as if waiting for my interjection, but I just nodded at what she'd said, and waited for her to continue. "We decided to do the décor as a nod to the conch-style houses found all over the Caribbean. The shortbread of the palm trees are orange, clove, nutmeg and cinnamon. We wanted to keep to island flavors." She pointed at the pastel icing on the front of the little cookies houses and the detailed white piping that looked exactly like the intricate wood designs that usually were done on the real life ones.

"They're so pretty, I almost don't want to eat them." That was Bobbie Halls, one of our female judges, who owned one of the most popular cookie shops in the country. Bobbie tapped on the steeple of the little church Sully had decorated. "This piping work is unbelievable; you even have a wreath on there. Well done," she said with a smile, and Sully beamed.

Jean-Georges grumbled in response then plucked one of the palm trees and snapped it in two. He nodded approvingly at the sound. "Good snap." He held up a finger immediately, a deep frown on his face. "But the flavor is the most important."

I held my breath as they each took a bite. Susan Park, our third judge, was the first to speak. "This is amazing. The lime and coconut are there, but the buttery nuttiness of the shortbread just melts in your mouth." That was high praise from a former White House pastry chef.

Jean-Georges never gave anything away, but when he went for a second bite, I almost sagged with relief. "Very good choice of flavors and the decoration is effective."

I spoke up then. "Sully did all the piping."

My baking partner widened her eyes at my interjection, and I could see a little bit of red blooming on her cheeks.

62

But instead of preening or saying something about herself, she looked straight at Jean-Georges and said, "Kiskeya did the pastry." My heart threw itself against my chest at her words.

"Well done, ladies," Bobbie said, as they went back to their chairs at the front of the studio.

I wanted to thank Sully for speaking up for me with Jean-Georges, but she just walked past me, gesturing toward the front. "Third challenge is about to start."

Within seconds, we were standing in front of the judge, ready for our last bake of the day. All the teams buzzing with nervous energy, despite the long day we'd already had.

Patricia stood by the judges as she gave us our instructions. "For the Showoff Showcase, we want you to make tree ornaments."

The appropriate oohing and aahing for the cameras followed more details. "We want four different flavored cookies that resemble traditional Christmas ornaments." She pointed at a table, which had appeared in the last few minutes. "This table has a bunch you can use for inspiration. We want a half dozen of each kind of cookie. You have three hours."

Sully rushed over to the table, and I followed her, trying hard not to look at the bounce in her ass as she ran. She immediately started grabbing stuff from the table. "Here," she said, shoving a glass snowflake in my hand.

"I like that one," I said, pointing at what looked like a little gift box with a big bow. "We can make petit fours for those. Maybe some curled candied orange for the bow."

Her eyes widened and went for it. "Good idea." She also grabbed a hand-painted red ball. "Some kind of rum ball or Russian tea cookie?"

More nodding from me, and on a whim, I grabbed what

looked like a sprig of mistletoe with a red bow. She widened her eyes at my impulse grab, but didn't say a word. That was probably for the best.

We got back to our stations, and immediately Sully had a pen and paper out. "Okay, petit fours for our gift box. What are you thinking for flavors?"

"Hot Toddy?" I suggested, and she nodded right away. Suddenly, I felt like my chest could take in air again.

"I like it, lemon sponge and maybe something spicy?" She was tapping the pen against her lips, and even in this moment of intensity—when there was no time for anything but focus—a surge of lust almost leveled me.

I looked at my reddened hands which had been burned more than once today, trying to get my head back in the game. "Four spice cake? Cinnamon, clove, nutmeg, star anise."

"Yes. I like it. How about doing the traditional Russian tea cake but blend in some turron?" The Spanish almond nougat would be a nice texture with the crumbly cookie, and it *was* a holiday classic. I almost smiled then, because despite our many run-ins, we worked well together.

"Okay brace yourself, for the snowflake, let's do a pizzele, but with a brittle on top. Cocada?" I almost said no to the Dominican coconut brittle, but I dipped my head in assent instead.

"That's fine. Ginger snaps for the mistletoe?

She crossed her arms like she was about to say something she knew would piss me off. "I've done this before, and it came out really good. A ginger snap and blend dried mango with chili into the batter." I thought about it, and I could see it working. The chewy texture would probably mix well with the crunchy cookie, and she'd done it before. It wasn't what I would've gone for, but as I had been reminded multiple times in the last two days, this wasn't the Kiskeya Show.

"Sounds good."

"You want to fight me on this so bad right now," she teased, aware of the fact that the cameras were always rolling.

"I do not," I protested, as I started to work. "Petit fours, Russian tea cakes, ginger snaps and pizzeles. I'll start on the first two, and you work on the others. We should have all these done in ninety minutes and then we can decorate. Equipo Sullkis al ataque." I said that last part as I lifted a flour-dusted fist up to her.

"You're not cute." Despite the grumbling, she tapped her fist to mine, and there was a tiny smile lifting up her lips. "Maybe your moody ass can finally embrace teamwork."

"I promise to try."

And I really would. Sully had shown me today she could put her feelings aside and do the work to win this thing. I had to step up and do the same. We had a shot at making it to day two, and I would do my part to get us there.

CHAPTER NINE

SULLY

"I can't believe you guys are not going to be in the kitchen anymore," I lamented into Alex's shoulder, tightening my arms around him.

He pulled back smiling sadly and gave me a kiss on the cheek. "We'll still be here all week. They were really awesome about letting us stick around if we wanted." He glanced up at Derek who was stoically standing by the door waiting for his teammate. "And we both have the time. We might as well..."

Alex's smile and the flush on Derek's face made it pretty easy to guess what they were going to be doing. My new friend gave me one last squeeze and moved to stand next to the massive blond who immediately draped an arm around him.

"Well, I'm glad someone gets to relax in this place for the rest of the week," I complained, and glared at Kiskeya who had said her goodbyes and had gone back to taking notes. About what, I did not know. We wouldn't even know what the second day challenges were until the morning.

"We're heading to bed. We're super tired." Alex

sounded way too wired for any sleep to be happening in that room, but I let them get away with the lie and wished them a good night.

By the time I closed the door behind them, Kiskeya had quietly slipped into the bathroom to take a shower. It had been a long-ass day, but I was still buzzing with nervous energy. I grabbed the bag of mango with chili I'd nabbed from the kitchen studio and got in bed.

I grinned when I saw all the texts from my mom and brother. I'd sent them a voice message after we finished, letting them know we'd moved on to day two, and warning them with pain of death against telling anyone or putting it on Facebook, since this wouldn't air until a couple of days before Christmas.

I shivered as I got under the covers, and then remembered I was in a fancy castle with a fireplace I could turn on with a remote. As soon as I got the fire going, my phone buzzed with a video call from my mom.

I accepted the call right away and grinned into the screen. "Mami. How long have you even been home?"

My mother had gone through a tough couple of years. After taking a bad fall at work that had shattered her shoulder, it took almost eighteen months and multiple surgeries for her to get back to normal. She'd been an engineer for one of the utility companies. One of the few women of color in her union. That job had meant the world to her, so losing her independence and ultimately her ability to do what she loved had taken a toll on her. She'd only been back to work for a few months and was still adjusting to being stuck indoors instead of out with her crew like she'd done for almost fifteen years. We were all still getting used to our lives being back to our new normal.

Her hair was short, almost a buzz cut, but it suited her—

my mother was all cheekbones. She was slim and tall, like Kiskeya. Because everything came back to Kiskeya today.

"Mija dime! Tell me how your day went. I'm so proud of you."

I shook my head at the phone. "Mami, you'd tell me the same exact thing if I'd lost."

She gave me one of her "don't sass me" clicks of her tongue. "I'm always proud of you. And I'm *extra* proud that you made it through. Not that I'm surprised; you're so talented and with another Dominicana," She widened her eyes like two Dominican women in Scotland at the same time was a major historic occurrence. "I mean, you're going to bring all the flavor."

If only my partner didn't seem opposed to every single idea I had. I turned to check Kiskeya's status in the bathroom, but it sounded like she was still busy in there. "She's been weird about using a lot of tropical flavors." I lifted a hand, remembering some of her confessions from the first day. "She does have her reasons, but today our most successful challenges were the ones where we actually collaborated. I hope she's more open to my ideas tomorrow, or we're going to butt heads."

My mother looked like she was ready to get on a plane and come give Kiskeya a talking to. "Ay no, and with that name. You'd think her family was all about the culture." I cringed, hoping the bathroom door was thick.

"She hasn't said much about her family." I didn't want to betray Kiskeya's confidence by sharing some of what she'd told me. "They're all still in the DR. She came on her own." I felt guilty even saying this. She seemed like such a private person, and I had a feeling she'd be mortified to hear me talking about her with my mom. So I changed the subject. "But we did these awesome shortbread casitas, Mami. You'll love them when you see the show."

"You didn't take any photos?" She sounded truly horrified.

"Nope." I laughed at all the teeth sucking on her end of the call. "I told you, we can't have any devices in the studio kitchen. They're really strict about nothing getting leaked until the show airs. But they came out great; they look just like the ones you have."

She smiled and turned her head, I assumed to look at her prized possessions. "That's nice, mija. What time is it over there?"

I looked up and saw it was close to 10:30p.m. "It's late." I let out a yawn that made my jaw crack. "I should get to bed, I'm—"

I was about to say tired when Kiskeya walked out of the bathroom in nothing but a black tank top and boyshorts, making all the blood in my body rush to my head. She had her hair up in her usual ponytail, but her skin looked flushed, like she'd turned the water up as hot as it would go. And Kiskeya looking supple and soft had a very intense effect on me.

"Sully." My mother's voice snapped me out of my staring.

"Mami. I'm gonna let you go. I'll check in on text tomorrow. Don't forget your stretches, okay?"

My mother's affronted face made me smile again, even as I kept my errant eye on Kiskeya's every move. "Who's the mom here? Tell Kiskeya hello for me. I started following her on Instagram. She's cute!"

I grinned thinking of the horrified look that would be on Kiskeya's face when I told her she had a new follower, and just then my teammate, who had been putting a long sleeve T-shirt on, turned her head in my direction.

"My mom says hi," I informed her, timing the punchline for when she turned back around. "She followed you on Instagram. She said you're cute."

She nodded without looking my way and kept riffling through her stuff. I went back to chewing on spicy mango and staring at her. I'd only counted to three when her head popped back up.

"Wait. She did what?" She look so pressed, I had to laugh.

"Relax, Kiskeya. She's not going to stalk you or anything. She's just super hyped about my baking partner being Dominican." I popped another piece of mango in my mouth and looked at the little bit of tight brown skin showing between her shorts and shirt. "You have to admit it's a pretty big coincidence."

She grabbed her phone from the chair where she'd left it charging and tapped for a few seconds. Then went back to whatever she was doing in her bag. I had to bite back a smile when she grumbled, "I followed her back."

After a few minutes of arranging and folding, she stood by the bed tapping more things into her phone, until I lost my patience.

"Who are you texting? Talk to me. I'm bored." I wasn't bored. Watching Kiskeya's wiry body flex, and the angular lines of her face as the light hit them were Grade A entertainment, but it was also not the healthiest distraction. And I wanted attention.

She finally looked up after another round of tapping and gave me a long look. "I'm not texting anyone. Just making sure I type up the things I can improve on tomorrow. We could've been more prepared for the actual challenge if we timed ourselves during practice."

It took a lot of strength not to roll my eyes at her. "Kiskeya." Deep breath. "*Relax*. We advanced. We got very good feedback in all the challenges."

"We got good feedback in two challenges; the first one was a disaster."

"We didn't have a single disaster today." She did not look convinced.

"No thanks to me."

"Thanks to our kickass teamwork." I was going to push a little bit, because I knew I wasn't imagining the energy in the room. "We're like the Carol Danvers and Maria Rambeau of the baking world." She pursed her lips, but I could see she was very close to cracking a smile, so I decided to shoot my shot. "Except more like the AO3 version because I'm like, really gay." With me, boredom usually led to extremely poor decisions, and I was in a mood.

She crossed her arms and smiled very grudgingly. "I'm clearly Carol in this scenario."

"Duh, Maria's the sensible one which, obviously would be me," I offered, then proceeded to crawl to the end of the bed where she was standing. The alarm on her face was almost comical.

"What are you doing?" Her voice was super high, her eyes widening as I got closer.

"Uh, getting cozier, so we can have a teammate heart-to-heart since you clearly need one."

She kept looking at me like I was a ticking time bomb. I was starting to get worried I'd pushed her too hard, until I realized she was staring at my boobs again. They pretty amazing, this was a fact, and she was looking at them like she wanted to dive right in.

"Stop glomming on my tits, Kiskeya." I thought that would make her look away, but she was looking more and more predatory by the second. I was feeling many feelings between my legs. So of course, I doubled down.

I sat on the edge of the bed with my thighs spread and leaned on my elbows so she could get a better look at the cleavage in question. "You were saying?"

"We were talking strategy, Sully." She sounded pissed, but she also grabbed the ottoman that was by the armchair and sat right in front of me. So close that our knees were almost touching.

I moved my head from side to side, considering her for a second. "You were talking strategy. I was eating mango with chili and staring at your ass." I said it while nudging her toe with mine, and she practically jumped a foot in the air.

"Stop. We're not doing this." I wasn't sure who she was trying to convince.

"Okay. We won't do *it*." I put a whole lot of emphasis on *it* and she swallowed audibly.

I kept looking at her, not even trying to hide that I was taking stock of all the places I'd put my mouth on if I ever got a chance.

"I never asked you what you would do with it." She quickly realized I could take that statement somewhere filthy very easily and added, "With the prize money, if we won. You asked me, but I never asked you."

It took my lust-filled brain a moment to get back online, because I'd been sure we were very close to getting busy, but Kiskeya played hardball. I had to close my eyes and legs (I wasn't a total mess), and focused on her question. This was for sure going to get us out of hard staring, dry mouth, and heavy breathing territory.

"I told my mom I'd use it to open an online business," I

said, sitting up. "My family owns a bodega uptown. In Washington Heights," I explained. "And a few years ago, when I was still in school, I started making pastries and people loved them. I'd post the daily offerings on Insta and people would just show and line up; it was wild."

Kiskeya leaned in, her eyes focused on me like she was hanging on every word.

"But my mom got hurt at work, and all of that had to be put way on the backburner. My brother takes care of the business, my dad did it before he died. But once he was gone my brother took over." My throat closed up thinking about my dad and how proud he'd be of me getting chosen for this contest. "Anyway, a lot of the savings went to covering medical stuff, even with my mom's insurance and worker's compensation. I'm sure you know, healthcare in the States is the shittiest and things add up."

"I'm sorry about your mom. Is she okay now?" Kiskeya being soft and compassionate was going to fuck me up.

"Yeah, she's much better. It was her shoulder, so it took a long time for her arm to heal, and she can't really do her old job. She's a fighter, though. But to answer your question, I'm supposed to use the money to start something of my own. A lot of people are doing good business in the city with deliveries. Postmates, Seamless, and shit. So it could work." I lifted a shoulder, back in the conundrum I'd had for the past few weeks. "But I wonder if I should just save the money for a rainy day or something. In case something else happens with my mom." The words came out of my mouth before I could even really think about them. I hadn't confessed that even to myself, and once I'd said it, I wasn't sure what to do with the realization.

"What would your mom say about that?"

I looked down, running a chipped nail along the piping

in my flannel pajama shorts. "She'd never let me do it. I mean, she would throw a full-on fit if I even tried it."

"You should let her know how you feel."

"Yeah, I guess," I agreed tiredly.

This time, she was the one who looked down at her shorts. "It's nice that your family's so supportive. Do they know?"

She didn't have to say what, we were both Dominican after all.

"She does. My dad had a harder time with it. He got a little too attached to a couple of boyfriends I brought around." I shook my head, remembering how extra he'd been. "But he eventually realized it wasn't a phase and got over it."

She nodded, eyes still fixed on the floor. "My family's definitely not over it. Not my parents at least. My sister and I are still close."

My heart ached for her. I knew how fucked things could get in Dominican families when people came out. I had my share of relatives who were still assholes about it. "Is that really why you left?"

She shrugged, still not looking at me. I wanted to tug on her hand and have her climb on the bed with me. Eventually, she looked up. "Partly. I dated a girl for a while in college, and I suspected they knew, or at least had an inkling, but they never said anything. After I graduated and decided I wanted to go to culinary school in the States, I told them." She laughed and it was not a happy sound at all. "Que desastre. I left not long after. We talk sometimes, but they've never come to visit, and I haven't gone back. My sister visits every year, though, and we talk a lot. She's very curious about you." That, she said with a genuine smile, but I was still not over the rest of what she'd said.

"I'm sorry, Kiskeya." I felt terrible for giving her such a hard time for being uptight and intense. It all made so much sense now.

"It's fine." I was about to protest when she retracted. "I mean, it isn't fine, it sucks, but I'm not going to change who I am."

"It's not fair." It sounded so stupid, like such a useless thing to say.

She didn't respond. Instead, she got up from the ottoman and went to the mini fridge in the room and grabbed two beers. She held up the bottles of Innis & Gunn —the Scottish beer we were all obsessed with since we'd arrived—and raised an eyebrow in question.

I assented and moved up to sit against the headboard. "Yes, please." I extended a hand, and she passed me the cold bottle then got into bed with me.

She clinked her beer to mine and took a long pull from it. I watched her drink and thought there were many things I'd discovered I found highly erotic in the past few days. Drinking from a bottle of beer was apparently one of them. When she finished, she licked her lips, and I almost had to press the bottle to my groin. "This beer is the best."

"Yeah," I croaked.

After taking another sip, she leaned on the headboard and turned her head to look at me. "You know what's the weirdest part about it?"

I shook my head as I took a drink from my own beer.

"I have an uncle that's gay, and even though it's not fully fine, he's still in the family. He even brings his partner to family stuff. And I'm not saying things are good for gay men in the DR, because they really aren't. But it almost felt like it was something that people could digest." She frowned as if she couldn't figure out how to explain herself.

"Like a guy wanting another guy made *some* kind of sense, but having no use for a man in any way? It was unthinkable."

"Fuck," I breathed out, leaning my head like she had and turning so we were face-to-face. "That makes so much sense. I mean with the toxic masculinity on steroids in the culture. Shit." I closed my eyes and felt so many things. I felt so close to her, like I understood. Really got what she'd done by telling her parents her truth, the risks she'd taken to live it. I was blown away by how brave she'd been to even try to be out, when it was clearly not very safe to do it.

I opened my eyes, and she was still looking at me, but her gaze was heated again. I could see the lust there. Immediately my body reacted to it. I wondered how long we'd tiptoe around this, how long I'd be able put off telling her exactly what I wanted. But like she'd been doing constantly this week, Kiskeya surprised me first.

"I want to kiss you so bad right now." She said it looking right at me. In that moment I knew the entire castle could've crumbled around us, and I would have been helpless to unlock my gaze from hers. She shifted, and I heard her bottle clatter as she placed it on the table. Her chest moved up and down like she'd been running. I hurried to put my own bottle down, almost dropping it on the floor, but soon my hands were free and I was kneeling on the bed in front of her.

Wanting. Wanting. *Wanting her.*

I ran my hand up her slender neck, placed my thumb right at her pulse point, and I could feel it racing. I was usually bold in moments like this, demanding what I wanted, but I didn't want ruin this. I wondered what she'd do if I climbed on her lap. If I straddled her thighs, pressing myself to her until she could feel my heat. I didn't ask.

Instead, I traced my finger on her earlobe, looked at the contrast of our skin together, her brown just a little darker than mine. I imagined us as little bits of soil, of earth, from the same place that had been picked up and scattered, and now were here, blending back together. Finding each other so far from where we'd come from.

"Sully." My name on her lips was a plea, a beckoning. I wasn't strong enough to hold back. I leaned in close until my lips were grazing her ear, and finally asked for what I wanted.

CHAPTER TEN

KISKEYA

"Besame, Kiskeya."

I knew this moment would come. From the minute I'd seen Sully walking into that room, I knew that given the chance, I'd end up exactly where we were now. About to plunge headfirst into a sea of bad decisions, and yet I was loath to stop. I turned so I was upright against the headboard and pulled her to me.

"Ven," I said. *Come.*

And she did. She spread her thighs over mine, making my hands itch to stroke her heat. To learn what she felt like, what she smelled like. I tipped my head up as Sully loomed over me, her eyes blazing. I placed both my hands on her hips, but before I slid them under her shirt, searching for all the treasure I'd been desperate to explore, I said what needed to be said.

"This is not the smartest thing we've done this week."

Sully kept her eyes on me and responded with a thrust of her hips. "I beg to differ. We're both stressed as hell. I was going to go to the bathroom and rub one out while I was pretending to brush my teeth. This is a much better solution."

I threw my head back and laughed. "You're too fucking much." She grinned back, a wicked gleam in her eyes.

"I think you like it."

I groaned in answer and slid the tips of my finger under her flannel shirt.

"Is this okay?"

She nodded, and I let my hands drift up her waist and belly until I was cupping her breasts. Her nipples were hard, and my mouth watered from wanting. I could feel myself getting wet, the need pulsing at my core, as I made her gasp from my touch.

"Mm, I can come like this." She said between lusty sighs, as I teased her a little, taking each nipple between my fingers.

"Like this?" I asked, feeling her hips circling harder with every pinch from my fingers.

"Yeah." She breathed out, with her hands braced on my shoulders. "Kiss me."

Her hips kept rocking back and forth in way that was driving me crazy. I slid one hand out from under her shirt, so I could bring her head closer. I wasn't shy or tentative about kissing, but I knew this one would be hard to come back from. I let myself feel the terrifying clarity that doing this with Sully could cost me everything.

I did it anyway.

I gripped a fistful of her hair as our mouths crashed together, my tongue stealing into her mouth, hot and hungry. I'd never really wanted before, I thought, not really, because this was incendiary.

"Mm," she moaned as she put both hands on my face and

licked into my mouth, the chili from the mango she'd been eating now on my tongue. She kept moving against me until she found the right spot. With every thrust, I could feel she was closer to coming. I wanted to see her face when she did.

"Sully," I whispered, pulling away to take a breath.

"Ungh, I'm so close. You got me so turned on. I want you to touch me." She took my hands in hers and slid it under her underwear until I was cupping her mons—the curls there ticking my palm.

"You're so hot," I gasped as I slid two fingers in, and kissed her hard. As I sucked on her bottom lip, I stroked her wet pussy, like I'd wanted to do for days.

"Like that, do it hard." I obliged and she let out a tortured moan and wrapped her arms around my neck and slid her tongue with mine. We were tangled together, locked in. And suddenly my entire purpose in life became making her fall apart under my hands.

She was wet from this, from our kisses, from my touch. I throbbed, needing relief too, but I couldn't do anything else but keep touching her until she was coming for me.

"I want to suck on this," I said as I circled the pad of my thumb on her clit. "I want to lick you. Spread your thighs with both hands and suck on that nub until you scream."

"Ahhh, don't stop." she pleaded against my mouth between hot, mouth wide-open kisses. "Tell me how you'll do it, how you'll eat my pussy." She was kissing my neck, teeth grazing the skin, and I was sure I was on fire.

"I'm going put you over the back of that couch and eat you out from behind until your legs give out." With every dirty promise I made, she thrust harder into my hand. I dipped my fingers in again and felt her pussy clench on them. I was going to come just from the sounds she was making. I almost used my other hand and gave myself some relief, but I wanted to wait.

"What are you doing to do after you make me come?" She was so close, I could hear it.

"I'm going to lay you on the bed and play with your tits, finger you until you come on my hand, and when I'm done, I'll sit on your face."

That was what did it. She stiffened and sucked hard on my tongue as her hips convulsed against me. I kept my hand on her mons, not wanting to leave her heat just yet, as we kissed lazily.

She spoke first, after she'd leaned back to look at me. She looked like a cat that ate all the cream. "I knew you'd be filthy." You would've thought she'd won the lottery. "And I'm going to let you know right now, there's no fucking way we're not doing this again, like, a lot over the next three days."

That hit me like a sucker punch. Fuck. Three days, *just three days*.

Sully's face changed too, probably realizing what she'd said, and immediately she went back in for another kiss. This time sliding us down the headboard until we were lying on the bed. She reached for the hem of my shirt, but stopped before taking it off. "May I?"

I nodded and went for the button on her shirt. She looked at me with an intensity I could feel on my skin and moved to lift my shirt over my breasts. "Kiske, I want you so bad." She just said things. Just let me know she wanted me.

I wanted to say things too. That I already was feeling too much. That I knew this "stress-relief strategy" was going to ruin me. But I kept unbuttoning her shirt instead. I slid it off her shoulders, my eyes fixed on her dark brown areolas. She'd been running her thumbs over my nipples, and the frissons of pleasure from her light touch made me shiver. I wanted to ask that she move her hands farther south, but before I could, her palm was making its way down my belly as she kissed my neck. "I wanna come together."

I nodded frantically, one hand already tugging at my sleep pants and underwear. "Take off your panties, Sully," I demanded and she complied. In seconds, we were naked and pressed against each other, her full heavy breasts brushing my smaller ones. I felt like every nerve in my body was about to combust.

When she finally got to where I needed her, she made a sound like she'd just unwrapped her favorite treat. My pussy clenched.

"Oh shit, you're bare."

I grinned at how reverently she ran her fingers over my Brazilian. "I live in LA. It might be a city ordinance." I joked as she kept caressing me.

With a grunt of appreciation the looked up, her face serious. "My regards to the city of angels."

I just shook my head at her and I brought my knees up to give her better access. "Put your mouth on me, Sully."

"What if I suck on your clit?" she asked hungrily, and again I was her prey. She sat up and I laid on my back, bare and open for her.

"Please," I begged, my heart skittering with anticipation.

She got on all fours and leaned in to kiss me, and I grabbed her ass hard with both hands, fingers digging in as she moaned. I let my hands roam to her clit, her ass. Touching her with an urgency that built almost by the second. Her hands roamed too, one finger in my mouth, a hand at the base of my neck, possessive, frantic.

I'd never had sex like this; it was primal and reckless

and I was already addicted. I kept fingering her, feeling my own pussy throbbing until I was ready to beg again. But before I could, she gave me one last kiss and crawled her way to where I needed her.

She lowered herself until her face was inches from my core. She glanced up and found me propped on one elbow, looking down at her.

"Glistening, and all for me." Her voice was reverent, making me melt into a puddle under her gaze. She used two fingers to spread my lips and blew on my clit. I sucked my teeth and threw my head back at the sensation. But still her mouth was not quite...there.

"Lick it," I demanded, as she slid the two fingers inside and nosed at the juncture of my thighs. "Come on, chula," I coaxed as I placed a hand behind her head.

"Do I have you dripping, Kiskeya?" she teased, as she ran the tip of her tongue on the edge of my labia, centimeters from my clit.

"You know you do. Come on, baby. I'm aching." That finally got me what I wanted, and when she started sucking on my clit, I sank into the bed, lost in what her mouth was doing to me. Within seconds, she had every nerve in my body on high alert. My entire world shrank down to what her tongue and fingers were making me feel, and the pleasure built and built. Radiating from my groin to my back, until my legs started shaking. When she pressed the flat of her tongue to my cunt and licked hard, within seconds my back lifted off the mattress, as I hoarsely screamed her name.

I must have lost time for a few seconds because when I came back to myself, her teeth were on my nipple, and she sounded smug. "Hey, look who's back."

"I think you broke me," I gasped, wrung out and entirely wrecked.

She laughed, and I risked opening one eye. I found her looking at me with a goofy smile, her lips a little swollen and bruised from her efforts.

"I think we should make this our reward for the hard work we're about to do for the next three days." Her tone was light, but I could see the weariness in her eyes. She expected a rebuff. For me to freak out and tell her I didn't want to risk our chances in the competition by getting caught up in this.

And I probably should have. Hell, I almost did. But when I reached for her, she came. When I kissed her mouth, it was musky with my taste, and her skin was hot like the island on summer days. I was not strong enough to say anything other than the truth.

"Why would we stop when we're so good at it?"

CHAPTER ELEVEN

SULLY

"We got this, chula," I said, as I bumped fists with Kiskeya and went to work. The last thirty-six hours had gone by in a blur of baking, planning for day two, and getting up to serious sexy times behind closed doors. Once we'd started, it seemed hard to stop touching, kissing, and so much more. My head was a mess of recipes and preparation times all swirling with images of the things Kiskeya and I had done to each other. This morning, I'd woken up to her kneeling in front of me, ready to give me a mind-blowing good morning.

I gazed at her as her fingers kneaded the dough for the two challah wreaths we'd be making for our Showoff Showcase, and felt goose bumps break out all over my skin. I recalled how those same fingers had teased and pleasured me for what felt like hours, getting me right to the edge, and then revving me up again until I'd come so hard, I'd almost passed out.

"Sully."

I almost severed my finger when she called me, I'd been so spaced out.

"Focus." Her tone was friendly, but her eyes were serious. She was in the zone, and I needed to get my shit together and stop fantasizing about her hands.

"Did you start poaching the figs?"

Fuck. I shook my head, already moving to the stove. "I'll start that now."

The last challenge today were wreaths, so we'd decided to do two of them. One savory and one sweet. Both with Mediterranean flavors. I was in charge of preparing the fillings for the honey and fig sweet wreath, as well as the sundried tomato, fontina, and pesto for the savory. We were hoping the ingredients would make the loaves look festive and that—of course—they'd taste great.

I left the figs poaching in the Madeira port and honey mixture and turned back to make the pesto. "Figs are on. Do you need help kneading?"

She looked up from the dough she was wrestling into submission and shook her head. "I'm good. Thanks."

I went back to my work, trying not to take it personally that she was back to acting like we were here to do a job together, and nothing else. Unlike me, Kiskeya didn't seem to be driven to distraction by what we'd been doing. I knew it was crazy to be wondering if there was a way to make this work after we got back to the States. But I did it anyways. I couldn't stop thinking about the possibility of her taking the apprenticeship in New York, if we won. Which we hadn't.

"The figs, Sully." Shit. I ran to lower the heat on the bubbling saucepan and focused on chopping basil and making the pesto.

I pointed at the mixture in one of the two food processors I had on the counter. "Is this good?"

She looked up from kneading and nodded. "Yeah, that's fine. I'm going to let this proof, then start the jam."

We worked in unison, anticipating the other's needs or moving in to help when more than two hands were required, and soon we were cleaning up our stations while the wreaths baked.

"Do you think we did enough?" Kiskeya asked as she rinsed one of the hooks from the mixer.

I looked up at her from the pistachio marzipan holly I was forming for the sweet loaf.

"They asked for one wreath and we're making two." I looked at the Beccas who also had their loaf in the oven, but seemed oblivious to the fact that cleaning up after themselves was an option.

More than once over the past few days, I'd wondered if those two were up to something. Because each time they'd ended up coming up with a flavor that was used by another team. First, it was the lingonberries that Derek had used in his Linzer cookies. Today, they'd used almost the same Asian flavors for their Panettone as Kaori and Gustavo had. They'd been horrible to everyone all week, so I wouldn't be surprised to find out they were up to some sneaky shit.

Kaori and Gustavo, on the other hand, were lovely, but seriously struggling. They were still running around, their wreath not yet in the oven. I cringed, wondering if they'd get it baked in time.

"We're fine. We did our best."

That was the wrong thing to say, of course. Kiskeya wanted to hear: "We're going to win."

But I didn't know when to keep my mouth shut, so instead of letting her fret in peace, I went right into the lion's lair. "Would you consider taking the job in New York City if we won?" There was no way to make that sound innocent, especially after she'd clearly told me the reason she was here was to get the job at *Farine et Sucre* in LA.

She made a show of looking at the time which said we still had another seven minutes for one and eight minutes for the other. Ten minutes left in the competition.

Nowhere to go, Kiskeya.

"If I didn't have any other choice," she replied with a shrug, and my face heated from embarrassment. "Why are you asking me that?" She took a long drink of a water bottle right after she asked, but I could see the red on her cheeks.

She was playing dense—my favorite.

So I reciprocated with brattyness. "No reason. Why would I care about you living in New York?" I kept my tone light, but we both knew her shitty answer pissed me off.

But that wasn't fair. I couldn't get mad because Kiskeya was going by the rules we'd agreed to. I'd been the one to suggest we could mess around while we were here and go on our merry way once we were done. I wanted to change things up, and that wasn't cool. I was going to fuck up our vibe with my neediness if I kept this up.

"Never mind; was just wondering." I gave her a smile I was sure made me look like I was in pain and turned my attention to the wreaths.

"Five minutes, bakers." That got us both moving.

The wreaths looked ready, so we got busy getting them plated for the judges. They came out beautiful and smelled heavenly. From behind us, we heard a crash and then Gustavo swearing in Spanish. Kiskeya glanced over her shoulder as I hurried to place the berries and holly leaves around the wreath after sprinkling it with powdered sugar.

She shook her head and whispered, "It fell apart on them."

Shit.

In the nick of time we got everything plated and ready. Soon the judges were waiting for our creations.

My heart pounded as Kiskeya and I walked shoulder to shoulder, each holding a challah wreath.

"Let's see how this tastes," Jean-Georges said, as he took a knife to one of the wreaths, and I could hear Kiskeya inhaling sharply. We explained what we'd done to them as they tasted.

"Oh my God, this is amazing." Susan always said that, but I still smiled gratefully.

Bobbie also seemed to love both flavors and complimented us on taking on the challenge of doing two. Jean-Georges gave us his usual stone face, but pinched off a second piece of the fig and honey, so I took that as a win.

Kaori and Gustavo were next and the judges were not as easy on them. Their Rosca de Reyes had not come together well, and in the end, it was under-baked.

The Beccas dazzled with some kind of pull-apart brioche wreath, so I wasn't surprised when Kaori and Gustavo were cut. The Beccas also managed to nab the thirty-minute advantage for the final challenge, since they'd been the team who'd finished first the most often throughout the competition.

I figured that Kiskeya would be shitty about losing to them, but she once again surprised me. She just winked at me and whispered, "We don't need it."

It was a bittersweet feeling. As elated as I was to go on to the final, I felt bad for our friends. But when Kiskeya turned to me and gave me a tight hug, all I felt was happy.

"To the finals, bonita," she whispered as the judges congratulated the Beccas and bid farewell to Kaori and Gustavo. I thought she'd let go after a moment, not wanting to attract attention. Instead, she pulled me closer and spoke quietly in my ear. "I'm going to take it so slow with you tonight. It's going to take me hours. I bet I can make you come just from sucking on your tits."

I gasped as she let me go, a pool of heat gathering between my thighs. She looked like pure mischief, making the doubts and reservations from the last half hour go up like so much kindle in the flames of my lust. I could lose my head for her. I had already started to.

I was ready to walk out of the studio and make a run for it in the direction of our room when Isla stopped us and called the Beccas over.

She gave me and Kiskeya a hug, but the Beccas just got a frosty smile. Not that I could blame her; they'd been treating her like the help the entire week.

And just to stay on brand, they rolled their eyes and slumped against one of the stations.

"What do you need? We're exhausted."

Isla was a real fucking trooper because she actually managed a smile. "I have your packages for day three. The secret challenge will be the first one this time. And the info for the other two is in the package." The Beccas took their packets without a word, glared at us, and took off.

We did the same after thanking Isla. Kiskeya and I stepped out of the studio into the cold Scottish night. It always felt weird leaving the studio, like we'd been in there for days. But tonight, there was a lightness to it, even if we'd had to see more of our friends leave the contest.

Scotland wasn't as cold as I thought it would be so far up north, and there wasn't really a lot of snow on the ground yet. But the stars seemed to all be out tonight. Kiskeya was quiet, like I'd noticed she'd been on the first day after the challenges ended. Probably going over everything we'd done today and how we could do it better next time. But I was caught up in the moment. That I was here with her.

She stopped next to me, and I felt her tip her head up too. "And to think, this is the same sky as in Santo Domingo." She contemplated and I searched for her hand. I wanted to feel connected to her, even if I knew I was getting dangerously close to corny.

She tangled her fingers with mine, and we looked up for a moment. Eventually I turned to look at her and said what was on my mind. "I'm glad I got to do this with you. I'm proud of us." We were representing our island here, and that felt monumental. But it was more than that. This experience had already changed me.

I stayed with my face lifted to the sky, hoping...but I didn't have to wait long. In the darkness of the Scottish night, she kissed me. It was short but thorough, and like all her kisses, piercing. She licked the seam of my lips as she tightened her hold on my hand. I parted them and her tongue stole inside, possessive, like she wanted to assert that these lips, this mouth, if only for tonight, were hers.

We pulled back, breathless, and I smiled at how serious she looked. "From looking at you right now, no one would suspect you just violated the sanctity of the kitchen studio by making filthy promises."

She grinned and I thought once again that walking away from this girl was going to hurt. "You know I'm a planner, Sully. I wanted to let you know what the program had in store for you after hours."

I had to laugh. "You're dirty."

"You like it, though." I could say no, but what would be the point?

I let her pull me along, and tried not to pay too much

attention to the pit in my stomach reminding me that we only had two more days together.

CHAPTER TWELVE

KISKEYA

"That's the thirty-five-grand winner right there," Sully gloated as she put the finishing touches on our practice cake for the last challenge of the competition. I stepped back from the workstation to take a good look at the coquito and passion fruit cake she'd made. The producers had given us access to the kitchen all day to prepare for the last bakes. We'd been in the studio along with the Beccas—who right now were working on the other side of a removable wall they'd placed as barrier—since the morning, and it was past dinnertime.

"I think we got this in the bag. That looks beautiful and it tastes even better." She came up to where I was standing and put her arms around my waist. "I'm proud of you, K. You finally went all in with celebrating our roots."

I almost shrugged it off, but it was true. I'd gone hard with the Caribbean flavors for this last challenge. Sully just kept nodding slowly and asking if I was okay this morning, when we were making our plan. The last Showoff Showcase's theme was "Santa Claus is Coming to Town" which was kind of all over the place, but I'd come up with the idea of a snow globe with a scene of a "Santa at the Beach."

We'd done a five-layer cake, and on top of it, we made waves out of meringues. We had spun sugar palm trees and made saffron and orange macarons. Those would be the gifts in Santa's sleigh. It was all encased in a sugar dome, and it looked pretty bomb.

"That Santa in board shorts you made out of modelling chocolate is kind of hot," she joked.

"You're ridiculous." I said biting back a smile while I looked at the screen of my phone which had been buzzing in my pocket. "Your mom just DMed me asking for a photo, by the way." Since we'd followed each other, her mom had gotten into the habit of getting to Sully through me. Because my teammate didn't remember where her phone was 90 percent of the time.

"I don't know where I left my phone, but she knows better. We can't send photos. Just tell her I'll call her later. Please, babe. I'll put the cake away while you do it."

I smiled at the "babe." She'd been calling me everything but my name since yesterday, and I had to admit, it was growing on me.

"Done." I pocketed my phone and kept looking at her as she moved around the room, putting all the things that we'd baked in a secured fridge.

"We have to remember to take our notebook too. We have all the designs and the notes in there."

She nodded, her back to me as she carefully placed our practice cake inside. "Yeah, because"—she lowered her voice for the next part—"the Beccas are slick as fuck."

"Right," I said distractedly as I looked at her bend down to adjust something in the lower part of the fridge. Her round ass became my entire field of vision.

She closed the door to the big fridge and turned around, a suggestive smiled bloomed on her lips as soon as she saw my face. "You see something you like, chef?"

I beckoned her to me in answer. "Ven aca, Sully."

The thought of what it would feel like to go back to LA and my small apartment shared with three roommates who I barely spoke to, tried to edge out the lust that was starting to swirl in my gut. But for once, I pushed it all aside and focused on the now, and how badly I wanted her.

When she came to me, I put my arms around her waist and kissed her deep, then pressed soft kisses to her jaw. "We're going to kick ass tomorrow." She tasted sweet from trying all the stuff we'd made, and it seemed like I would never get enough.

There were moments when these last few days seemed like they'd been an entire lifetime. That Sully and I had made our own world here.

"We make a good team." she said, as she planted kisses on my neck and face, making me shiver.

"We do." I gave her more access to my neck, as I moved my hands down to her ass. "You came up with the idea for the sticky toffee pudding soufflé. I think we're going to blow their minds with that."

Sully preened and went back kissing every inch of skin she could get to. She kept talking between licks and nips. "And don't forget the Whisky Cream semifreddo. That's where my badassery really jumped out."

"I need to be very thorough today in showing my gratitude," I promised as I dipped two fingers into her heat.

Sully groaned, pressing herself tightly to me. "Can you give me a preview now? Because kitchen sex is kinda one of my ultimate fantasies."

It was like she'd discovered the button inside of me

ADRIANA HERRERA

where my unbridled lust lived. I'd lost count of the times
we'd come together in the last couple of days, and every
time we did, it just seemed to make me want her more. I was
addicted to the way Sully tasted, how she moved. The way
she sounded when I made her come. Like it wouldn't occur
to her to hold back, to not show me, *tell me* what I did to
her. In an instant, I had her up on one of the counters in the
kitchen, kissing her hard, my hands on her breasts.

Her nipples were hypersensitive, and she could come
just from me playing with them. I was obsessed. I pinched
and worried one while I kissed her neck. When she let out a
moan, I pulled back, extracting an outraged balk in
response.

I made a zipping motion across my mouth. "We have to
be very quiet." I pointed at the wall. On the other side, we
could hear the music the Beccas always had playing. I came
close again and kissed up her neck until I was talking
against her mouth. "If you can't keep it down, your dream of
kitchen fucking will not come true." I had no idea where
this raunchy version of me had come from, but for Sully, she
was always on tap.

She put a finger over her lips. "Shhh, I'll be super quiet,
babe, I promise. But I need you," she whispered urgently,
followed by more soft nibbles and kisses. Her hand blindly
guiding mine to her wet pussy. She was always like this,
ready, wanting. Sometimes it felt that if given the chance, I
could lose days caught up in her.

I stepped back after one last bruising kiss and pulled her
ass closer to the edge. "Let me see what this mighty need is
all about." I looked up for a second and waved a hand at the
counter. "Hold on." She gripped the edges, lips red and
swollen, as her eyes followed my every move.

This was crazy, reckless, and other than a fire or a

96

natural disaster, I didn't think anything would be able to stop me. I went down on my knees so that my mouth was exactly at her crotch. I brought my eyes up and discovered she'd closed hers, already lost to what she knew I'd give her. "Babe, please."

I nosed her cunt over the thin fabric of her leggings, smelling her. Her scent had been stuck to my hands for days, and I was loath to even think of what it would be like to lose it. I mouthed her moisture and she bucked forward, needy.

"Stop teasing me." she pleaded through gritted teeth, and brought one hand to the back of my head.

I leaned back and tipped my head up to look at her. "But you haven't said what you want."

"You. I want you." There was some kind of primal thing that happened to me whenever she got like this, her voice reedy and just a little desperate. Like only I could give her what she needed. I pressed my open mouth to her crotch and tongued over the fabric, trying to coax out more pleas. "Take them off. Off," she demanded and I obliged.

I pulled on her leggings as she pushed her ass off the counter, and a few tugs later, I had them down to her ankles, her slick pussy at eye level. My mouth watered from how much I wanted her. I pressed my face closer, one hand on her thigh, the other spreading her labia, so I could see all of her.

"I can't stop thinking about this pussy." All I got was a tortured groan in answer. I ran my tongue up and down a couple of times, and I could taste her wetness. "It's so sweet. Can't get enough." I pressed my mouth to her clit, worrying it with my tongue, until I had her panting.

She moved one hand to cup the back of my head. "More." Her voice was tight with need, and it only made me want to work her up more. I ran the pads of my thumb along the inside of her pussy as I sucked on her. Her hips circling wantonly. "Ah, don't stop, K." There was nothing on earth that could make me.

I flicked the hard tip of my tongue against her pussy and put my hands on her ass to push her tightly against my mouth. After a few moments I felt her lose her balance and heard a crash by my head.

"Shit," she said distractedly, as I redoubled my efforts, already feeling her legs start to tremble.

"Is everything okay over there?" It took me a second to register it was one of the Beccas calling from their side of the wall.

I was about to answer but Sully kept my head right at her cunt, a stern look on her face. When she spoke, it was barely a whisper. "You better finish what you started, Kiskeya Burgos." I grinned as I went right back to work and she lifted her head in the direction the Beccas' question came from. "We're fine, just cleaning up." The last word was more of shudder, as I hit a particularly sensitive spot.

"I'm close, babe," she said, as I lifted my eyes to her. She had her head thrown back, quiet moans escaping her lips. Within seconds, she was coming, her clit hardening with every flick of my tongue until she was spent. I pressed kisses to her mons and the inside of her thighs as her breath came back to normal.

After a moment, I helped her get her clothes back in order and pushed up, so I could kiss her. She shook her head as we pulled apart. "It drives me a little crazy whenever I smell myself on your lips."

"You make me wild Sully Morales." I wasn't sure if I was telling myself or her.

She put her arms around my neck and went in for

another kiss. "I'm feeling pretty wild myself, but I think we should get out of here, before we really get caught."

I laughed at the close call with the Beccas and helped her down from the counter.

"Let's go."

Only when we were back in our room, ensconced in the cocoon of our bed, did I get the niggling feeling we'd forgotten something back at the kitchen. But by then, nothing could've gotten me away from Sully's warmth.

CHAPTER THIRTEEN

KISKEYA

At first, I couldn't really tell what the Beccas were doing, since we were standing by the sidelines waiting for their thirty-minute advantage time to run out. But when Patricia went to ask what they were making Rehbecca with an H looked straight at me, a shit-eating grin on her face, and said in a very clear voice, "We're making a snow globe."

I felt Sully stiffen next to me, but when we saw her pull out a sketch that looked eerily familiar to ours, I felt the blood in my veins go ice cold.

I watched in horror as she explained to Patricia they were doing a Santa scene under a sugar dome to give the effect of a globe, I recalled what we'd gotten up to last night. We'd been in such a hurry to get out of the kitchen we'd left our notes behind. I knew I should've been more careful. That the Beccas were devious and had been quite possibly cheating all week. But once I was in the room, in bed with Sully, I'd forgotten the reason I was in Scotland in the first place.

All week, I'd been relaxing my boundaries, letting go of

my focus until I literally screwed myself over. All my career plans, even my chance to stay in the States, were tied to this win, and I had most likely blown it.

My heart pounded with the realization that our entire plan was a bust. Because today, it was coming down to this final bake. We'd taken the second one with the soufflé, but we'd fucked up on the first challenge. So we were neck to neck, and now we were fucked.

If we did the same design as the Beccas, we'd be the unoriginal ones. We'd be the ones who copied their idea. And it's not like we could accuse them of ripping us off. What could we say? "They took my design last night, when I rushed out after doing my teammate in the practice kitchen."

"We need to do something else," I whispered frantically to Sully who was still frozen in horrified realization, staring in the direction of the Beccas' workstation.

I glanced up at the clock, and I felt like I was going to throw up. We had twenty-five minutes to figure out a new plan, or we were doomed.

Sully glanced at the clock too and turned slightly green. "We can't just do something different, Kiskeya. There's no time." She was speaking so low that it was barely audible, but her annoyance at me came through loud and clear.

"I'm not doing the same thing as them!" My voice went way higher than appropriate, so much so that Patricia came over to talk to us.

"Are you ladies all right?" she asked, looking between us. I was having trouble keeping the panic in check and thankfully Sully spoke up first.

"We just need to hammer out last-minute details." If I hadn't spent the last few days examining every single one of her smiles, I wouldn't have been able to tell she was close to falling apart. "Can we take five?" she asked, her eyes back on the countdown clock.

I was blown away at her ability to keep a calm demeanor. I was certain if I opened my mouth, I'd start screaming and never stop, or throw up and then burst into tears.

Patricia could tell something was wrong and scanned the studio for a moment. The judges came and went during the challenges and were only there for the first and last bit. After considering the situation and taking another close look at the two of us, she leaned and whispered, "You can step into the second pantry, but make sure you're back at least five minutes before you start. They'll want to film as the clock winds down for you." We both nodded and hurried to the small room where they stored extra supplies to replenish the pantry in the studio.

As soon as we got in, I started pacing the tight space, while Sully looked on, her arms crossed tightly against her chest. An image of last night came to me, of how she'd laid on the bed smiling as I pressed kisses to her belly. But right now, the memory made me sick with guilt. "This is a nightmare. I knew I'd forgotten something last night," I said through gritted teeth. "But I was so fucking...caught up in—"

She did move then, stepped right in my way and looked up at me defiantly. "Don't say it, Kiskeya. If you do, you can't unsay it and you'll regret it later." I felt resentful that Sully, who always seemed to be all emotion, was calm now. Cool and collected when I felt like I was mentally flying apart.

I almost laughed at the irony that in the moment of truth, I was the one losing control. "We will lose, Sully. Don't you don't get it? This is it." I threw up my hands, as if she wasn't understanding me. I opened my mouth and closed it, one time, then two, and finally I just said it.

"This is my only chance at getting my work visa extended," I said, choking on my own stupidity. "This was my long shot at actually staying in the States, and if I lose, I'm out of options."

"What?" She looked stricken, like I'd slapped her across the face. "You didn't say anything. I knew you wanted to win, but I thought it was just, you know, a stepping stone and that it was great just to be here. That either way it would be okay."

"You always think everything's going to be fine; it must be nice to be able to ignore reality," I scoffed.

"Why didn't you tell me?" she asked, tears brimming in her eyes, and I ruthlessly smothered the need to comfort her.

"I just met you, Sully. This isn't your to fix," I said, pressing a palm to my chest. "*I am not your problem.*"

She flinched at my words; they hurt her, like I meant them too. "I would've been more helpful. Not distracted you."

I sighed, looking up at the metal ceiling. "I did school for a couple of years and had a student visa. I was able to work for another year, but my work visa is running out this spring. The apprenticeship would buy me another year. This is a fucking nightmare."

She shook her head, and I hated that I'd made her regret what we'd done, what we'd been to each other. Because no matter how scared I was right now, I couldn't make myself be sorry for that. I should've told her that. Instead, I turned away from her. But when she could've lashed out, of hurt me like I'd done to her, she stepped up.

"We need to think fast, then. We have ten minutes.

'Santa Claus is Coming to Town' is the theme. We can still go with Santa in the Caribbean."

This all sounded fucking ridiculous, but I had to get it together. I nodded, and she kept talking. Taking notes on a pad she produced from somewhere in her apron. "We can still do the sleigh. The cake can be a present."

I made an affirmative noise as ideas ran through my head. "We can do a choux. Saffron with an orange blossom filling, with a honey craquelin."

"Yes. That's good; that combination worked well last night. Macarons?" she asked, as she wrote more stuff down.

"Sure, yeah those can be more gifts."

She looked up, her eyes clear and earnest, like I hadn't cut her to the core. "I can make vanilla bean with a spiced rum filling."

"All right. I can make the sides of a sleigh with coconut nougatine," I said, the image forming in my head, of a sleigh full of tropical treats.

She dipped her head again, as she wrote more notes. "I'll make the cake and macarons. You do the cream puffs and the reindeer from modeling clay? You're better at that." I felt my face heat at the compliment. I didn't deserve her kindness.

She looked at her watch and started moving toward the door. "We have three minutes. Let's go."

"Sully." I tried to touch her before we went back outside, but she shrugged me off.

With a hand on the doorknob, she spoke without looking at me.

"I don't ignore reality, Kiskeya. I just choose to be grateful. And maybe that makes me stupid. It's true that I could take my own dreams more seriously. I'm trying to. And yes, I got caught up in you in these past few days, perhaps more than I should have, but I don't regret it. I wanted you, and it made me happy, so I let myself have that. I'll never be sorry, even if you are."

"I never said I was sorry," I protested, hearing the tears in her voice and hated myself for causing them.

"I will do everything I can to help us win." And that was the last time she spoke to me like I wasn't a stranger.

The next three and a half hours passed in a blur.

We toiled to the very last second. I made the choux, modeled perfect reindeer out of chocolate, complete with sunglasses for the Caribbean sun. Sully made a five-layer cake with a gorgeous coquito sponge that tasted like coconut cream, cinnamon, and nutmeg with a passion fruit curd filling that looked almost too good to eat.

When Patricia called time and the judges exploded in applause from their table, we both stepped back in a daze. It was over, and in the end, we'd made something that was truly spectacular. When I turned to look at the Beccas, I could see the fury in their faces. We had out-baked them.

Within minutes, the judges were asking us to bring our showcases forward. The Beccas went first. The judges pointed out that the idea was great, but seemed rushed. *No shit.* But that they'd delivered on the flavors. They didn't look happy, and I felt too sick with worry about our own judging to gloat.

When it was our turn, Sully and I hefted the heavy dessert up to the judges and stood side by side, waiting.

Bobbie spoke first. "Santa in the Caribbean." She grinned as she looked closer at the wayfarer-wearing reindeer. Just two, because I only had so much time. "This is incredible. The nougatine is really holding up." She turned to us, pointing at the cream puffs. "Saffron and orange?"

We both answered at once: "Yes."

"Bold," Susan responded as she picked one up. "I need a taste."

Jean-Georges was next, a knife in hand, poised to slice into Sully's perfect cake. "Tell me about this."

Sully looked at me, and I nodded. It was her cake, she should talk about it. Besides, I was too overwhelmed to make any sense.

"It's a coquito and passion fruit cake. Coquito is a Puerto Rican holiday drink, similar to eggnog, but it's made with coconut cream, rum, and spices." She brought up her hand and started ticking fingers as she went. "Nutmeg, cinnamon, clove, and I made a passion fruit curd for the filling." She glanced up at me, a smile still on her lips, but it was barely a shadow of the radiant ones I'd been gifted with this past week. "We hope you like it."

I felt short of breath, suffocating in my own regret as I stood there.

Jean-Georges just groaned in answer as he cut into the cake. Soon, they were all taking bites. Susan and Bobbie nodded as they chewed, and when Bobbie spoke, she could barely contain her smile. "I am going to steal this!" She teased.

Susan concurred, as she nibbled on the cream puff. "This is glorious. The combination of flavors is genius. Wow."

Jean-Georges held one of the macarons in his hand, inspecting it closely. He held it to his nose. And then presented it to us. "Bourbon vanilla and spiced rum?"

I dipped my head. "Yes, chef."

He bit into it, chewed slowly, and swallowed, his expression impassive, and I was sure I'd pass out if he didn't say anything. After another long pause, he finally spoke. "Bon."

With that, he walked away, the macaron in his hand, the others trailed behind him to go make their decision.

I could see Sully's chest expand as she took a deep breath, and I wished I could throw my arms around her, kiss her. Tell her how proud of us I was, but she walked off without saying a word. Still, I had to thank her. I hurried behind her, as we walked out of the studio to take a ten-minute break and freshen up before the judges came back with their verdict.

"Sully," I called, the urgency clear in my voice. "Thank you." It was such a weak fucking thing to say when this week, she'd given me everything, but it was all I had. "Just... thank you."

She looked at me like she didn't know me, her shoulders tense. "You don't need to thank me, Kiskeya. I didn't just do this for you. I wanted to win. I wanted to do well. The difference between us is that I don't need to treat other people like shit to do it." She walked down the hall and out of the studio without a backward glance. I stood there realizing no matter what the outcome was, I'd already lost.

CHAPTER FOURTEEN

KISKEYA

We won.

The judges came back and announced we were the new Holiday Baking Challenge champions. Our friends who had stayed after they'd been eliminated were there to cheer us on. We smiled for the cameras, embraced stiffly at the request of the producers, and the whole time, I was numb. I kept checking to see where Sully was, fearful she'd disappear before we had a chance to talk things out. After filming ended, the crew brought in champagne and plates so everyone could taste the desserts. Everything could've been sawdust for all that I could taste it.

People kept coming up to congratulate me, to tell me how great we'd done, but all I wanted was to get out of there. Go back to our room and talk with Sully. Tell her I was sorry. Tell her how I felt. The need to do that became more urgent by the second, but every time I was about to do it, someone got in my way. I had my eye on Sully who was standing by one of the exits talking with Alex, and decided this was my chance.

"Kiskeya la Bella y campeona." Gustavo came up to me

with a big grin on his face and gave me a tight hug. "I can't say I didn't want to win, but seeing you beat those two was almost as good."

I did my best to smile, keeping an eye on Sully. "Thanks, Sully was the one that kept us on track."

He shook his head like I was being ridiculous. "Nah, I was watching. You two are like a symphony together. Completely in sync." I closed my eyes when he said that, choking down the sob threatening to escape my throat.

"Is everything okay?" I rubbed my eyes trying to keep the tears from falling. I couldn't even remember the last time I'd cried, and it was such a mindfuck. Here I was, with everything I'd been working for the last three years to get, and I was...bereft.

When I opened my eyes Kaori, Derek, and Gustavo were all standing in front of me looking worried. "I'm fine." I was so obviously not, but I didn't have time to explain. "I just need to talk to Sully. If you guys will excuse me," I said, trying to get past them.

Derek frowned and turned to look in the direction of the exit, as if a realization just dawned on him. "She and Alex went back to the castle. She said she needed help in her room."

As soon as he said it, I hurried out of the studio. "I have to go, sorry."

"Ms. Burgos!" I came to a dead stop just as I was about to reach the door that would take me outside and to Sully. I recognized Jean-Georges's booming voice before I turned to see him.

"Chef," I said, trying my best not to squirm. I must have been losing my mind, because this could be the most important conversation of my career and the only thing running through my head was: *I need to get to her. I need to get to her.*

"You are a very deliberate baker. You also appreciate the traditional flavors. The classics are *classics* for a reason."

I swallowed and nodded again, bristling at his words. Words that a week ago would have been the greatest compliment for me. But now, after Sully, I felt like a fake. An imposter trying to sell out my roots for this man's approval.

"You are the winner, so the offer to come on as a sous chef at *Farine et Sucre* is open to you. It's a great opportunity. I am sure you know this. At Farine, you will learn to bake like one of the masters." I wondered how long it would be before I hated myself and my baking? Until I smothered everything about me that was real.

I gulped down the "no, thank you" which practically crawled out of my throat and did my best to smile. "I appreciate the offer, sir. It's a dream opportunity for any young chef."

He looked at me curiously, obviously confused by my lack of enthusiasm. Maybe he expected me to bow down and kiss his hand. But when I thought about what I was feeling, the relief that should've been there at the confirmation I would have a job wasn't there. After years of hustling, of staying three steps ahead just to keep this dream going, I finally had a concrete plan for the near future, and it didn't seem to matter just then. There was something more important I needed to do.

"Thank you again. If you'll excuse me. I have to go." I left him standing there and ran as fast I could to the castle.

As soon as I made it to our room, I knew. I walked in and saw her bags were gone. Her pajamas, which had hung behind the bathroom door were not there. The book she'd been reading was not on the bedside table.

I wiped the tears streaming down my face and got my phone out of my pocket.

I tapped on it, barely able to see the screen.

Kiskeya: Te fuiste.

After a few seconds, she replied.

Sully: I left. You got what you came for Kiskeya—you won. And I got what I needed, a reminder that after the last couple of years, I can still be me.

Kiskeya: I didn't get to say goodbye.

Sully: I didn't want to make you. It would've hurt too much to hear you say you could go back to LA like the last few days had meant nothing.

My heart was pounding and my hands felt cold, like all the blood had sucked back into my heart.

Kiskeya: It meant everything. Everything. And I hate that I didn't get to say it to you.

Sully: It meant everything to me too.

When my next few messages went unread, I sank to the floor of the half-empty room and cried. I'd always prided myself in never wasting an opportunity. I always seized any chance I was given, capitalized on it, made it work for me. I'd left my family, my island, my whole world to go looking for the life I thought I deserved.

But these last few years, I'd gone further and further into myself. I didn't let myself enjoy the wins, always focusing on what was next. What Sully said was the truth— I had forgotten to be grateful. To let the joy of a moment fill me up.

What good was any of this if I had no one in my life to share it with? What good was all this work if I lost myself in the process? What did any of this matter if when I was handed happiness, I couldn't even recognize it?

Eventually I stood and started gathering my things. I wouldn't sleep in that bed without her. With every second that passed, the reality of what this week had meant for me grew in its intensity. I was folding clothes and shoving them in my bag when my phone vibrated. I quickly picked it up, thinking it might be Sully, but it was a message from her mom.

Magalys: Felicidades, Kiskeya. I hope you two figure things out. Take care, querida.

I felt tears stream down my face again at the kind words. Sully had only brought goodness to my life. I didn't know what I'd done to deserve it, but I vowed right then and there that I would put it all on the line to make sure she knew that.

CHAPTER FIFTEEN

SULLY

New York City, Christmas Eve

"Ay, mija, I'm not sure it's a good idea to leave you alone all day." I gritted my teeth at my mother's third attempt to cancel her trip to the outlet mall so she could monitor my moping.

I counted to three before I responded, because I knew she was just worried about me. But in the week since I'd gotten back from Scotland, I'd barely had a moment to myself and I needed some breathing room before I exploded.

My mother was outside of the glass counter of the family's bodega. Usually my brother was the one running the store, but today we only opened for a few hours and I'd offered to stay while they trekked up to one of the outlet malls in the suburbs.

"Mami, I'm fine. En serio, stop worrying. You know I hate the mall, and I have all the business from this morning to go over." I pointed at the screen of my laptop where I'd been reconciling all the orders clients had picked up last night and this morning for their own Christmas Eve parties. "I have to do all the bookkeeping, and we're only open for like four hours today. Don't worry. Go." I waved a hand in the direction of the street.

My mother didn't look too convinced. I had been a mess when I got back. Blessedly, I'd come home to a bunch of requests for cakes and pies from costumers in the neighborhood and the round-the-clock baking had taken my mind off Kiskeya. Except that was a lie, because I'd thought about her nonstop. Especially when all the promo and shit for the show had started popping up on the Cooking Channel. My heart felt like it would burst every time I saw her. It hurt.

Kiskeya had contacted me a few times to ask how I was. To make sure I'd made it home okay, but I'd kept it short. I was still too raw.

My mother clicked her tongue and walked around the counter toward me. "Ay, Mamita. You're just so sad. You haven't even said what you'll do with your prize money."

I hated that I was worrying my mother. But it had only been one week and I still had no clue how I felt about anything.

It had been a shock to leave the castle and with each mile, my heart broke more. In just a few days, I'd fallen hard for Kiskeya. I didn't know what to do with that. I missed her. I wanted her. But it was impossible. She was in LA, finally living the dream she'd worked so hard for, and I was here, still figuring out what was next.

I ran a finger along my mother's hairline and smiled, feeling the depth of her love. Even when she drove me a little nuts with her worrying. "It's only been a week, Ma. Give me a little time. I'll figure it out."

She kissed my cheek and hugged me tight, and I let

myself sink into it. "You don't have to rush, mi amor. You take the time you need. I just wish you would talk to her."

I shook my head hard at that. "What's the point, Mami? She's there and I'm here."

We'd gone over this a hundred times in the last week, and my mother still seemed unfazed by the fact that Kiskeya had not only expressed zero interest in having a relationship with me, but lived and worked on the opposite side of the country.

Still, she seemed to be mollified a bit by how agitated I got. I knew she'd be back at it later, but for now, she grabbed her bag from under the counter, mumbling about "stubborn muchachas."

"Your brother and I will be back around 3:00 p.m." she said, pointing to the door where I assumed he was parked. "Your tio needs the car back to go up to White Plains to his mother-in-law's." She crossed herself at the mention of my uncle's very cranky relatives by marriage. "Thank goodness she stopped inviting us after I got into that fight with her after the election."

I laughed at that and waved goodbye as she headed out. But before she pulled the door open, she turned around and surprised me with a question. "You love her, don't you, mija?"

The tears should've been answer enough, but somehow I managed to get out, "I think so, Mami, but I'll get over it eventually." I gulped a couple of times, feeling ridiculous. But my mother had always taken her children's feelings seriously. She came back and leaned over the counter to kiss me on the cheek.

"You shouldn't have to get over it. It'll be all right. *You'll* be all right."

I nodded, not sure what to even say and watched her walk to the waiting car.

The store wouldn't open for another hour at 9:00 a.m. I had just enough time to go over the last of the receipts before the entire neighborhood came through getting last-minute things for their Nochebuena dinner plans. I'd been working on my receipts for a bit when I heard a knock on the glass door. I ignored it at first, used to some of our regular customers' bad habit of coming by too early or too late and expecting service. But when a second round of tapping disrupted the math I was trying to do, I went to see who it was.

As soon as I got a clear view of her, I froze. I was rooted to the spot five feet from the door. She looked the same and yet so different. And I realized it was because I'd only ever seen her in Scotland. And now here she was in my city, on my block, outside my family store...and I wasn't sure I'd be able to find out why because I was going to black out.

Breathe, Sully. Respira.

I took the two steps to the door like I was floating. I grabbed the handle and looked at her for one more second before opening the door.

"Sully." She said my name in Spanish, like always. There were ways in which my name could be said properly and still be in English. Still sound Anglo, but she said it in a way I felt in my soul. Like my people said it.

She walked in and I stepped back, still not talking. I didn't know where to start.

But I was me, so I gripped my hands together in front of me to keep from grabbing her and said exactly what was on my mind. "I'm not going to ask dumbass questions because I obviously know why you're here." I'd been so focused on her face, on taking all of her in after thinking I'd never have her this close again that I didn't notice what she was holding in her hands. And when I did, despite myself, I smiled. "You brought me chili mangos and a bouquet of mistletoe."

She dipped her head, face still solemn. "I figured it couldn't hurt."

"You're not funny," I retorted, taking the offerings from her hand.

"I'm not trying to be. I missed you." Her voice broke on the last word, and I almost gave in, but I had to hear it.

I put a hand up and closed my eyes, trying to gain some composure. "You need to say it, and not why you're here. I know this is a grovel." I opened my eyes in case she tried to deny it, but she didn't. "I want to know what your plan is, Kiskeya. You don't do a damn thing without thinking ten steps ahead, so don't tell me why you're here now. Tell me what happens after."

Her face crumpled for a fraction of a second, but she got it back together. She had bags under her eyes, and her already-slim face seemed even leaner. It was a bittersweet relief to know I hadn't been alone in my misery.

Her throat convulsed, and I could tell she was having trouble with whatever she had to say. I didn't want to look away, but I could tell whatever was coming out of her mouth next was going turn me inside out, so I panicked.

"Wait, let me put this down." I ran to the counter, gently placed the bouquet and bag of dried mangos down and came back. By then, she was shaking her head, a watery grin on her face.

"I missed you so fucking much."

I wasn't talking until she said what she came all the way here to say. I was worth her laying out her heart.

"I start a new job January second."

I dipped my head and looked at my feet. "Yeah, your dream job."

Her hand reached for mine, and in the smallest voice I'd heard from her, she asked, "Can I?"

I gripped her fingers immediately, and I could've wept to be holding her clammy hands again. "I was hoping you would give me the rundown on a Dominican's first New York winter survival guide."

And because I had no fucking chill, I screamed. "You did what?" My hands and my feet went rogue after that, and in an instant I had both arms around her neck. "Tell me, Kiskeya."

"I turned down the job at Farine. I took the one here in New York, at Canela."

My lips were practically burning to smash against hers, but I resisted, because there was shit that needed to be said.

"You gave up your dream job, the only reason why you were even in Scotland. Your life goal."

She shook her head, and with each swivel, her mouth inched closer to mine. "First of all, I'm an idiot. Second, I may have gotten there with one life goal, but I left with a completely different one."

"But what about your visa? I've been worried sick about that."

"I'm sorry I worried you, mi amor."

My back stiffened at the words. She'd just said, *my love.* "Don't play with me, Kiskeya."

"Oh, I'm dead serious. If you want space, if you want time, even if you don't want anything to do with me, I needed to do this. I had to try. Sully, you brought home back to me. My roots, my core, the things that make me *me,* and on top of that, you gave me this." She said that last part as she pressed us closer. I put my nose on the crook of her neck and inhaled, feeling like my lungs could fill up for the first time since I left that castle in Scotland.

"You're giving up a lot, Kiskeya. What if you change your mind?" I asked, not wanting to believe this could be really be real.

"I've never been more sure of anything than I am about this." She pulled back so she could find my gaze, holding it as she spoke. "Do you want to hear how I knew?"

"Tell me."

"It was the first time ever I didn't have to wonder what came next. The only thing that mattered was being here with you."

A sob escaped my throat and I tightened my arms around her neck until our noses were pressed to each other. "Fuck this, I need to kiss you."

She grinned and I pounced. I kissed her like I'd imagined I would during all these days when I thought I'd lost her. I kissed her like she was exactly what I'd needed and thought I'd never be able to have again. After what felt like hours and not nearly long enough, I pulled back.

"I have so many questions..."

She pressed her lips to mine again, lingered there, until I almost swooned. "I only have one."

"Yes." I grinned as she laughed against my mouth.

"I didn't ask yet." Another soft kiss, and then her mouth moved across my face until her lips were grazing my ear. "Will you let me court you, Sully Morales?"

I shuddered out a shaky breath, because she was going to wreck me forever. "Does that mean we can't do it? Because I really hope you have a hotel where we can go as soon as I can lock this place down."

That husky laugh against my ear was breathing life into me. It was like my entire body was a plant getting watered for the first time in weeks. "I do have a hotel, and things are definitely getting done there."

"Thank God."

Her shoulders shook at my relief, and after a moment, she filled me in. "The show's setting me up for a couple of weeks. Hopefully I can find a place to live by then. The manager from Canela said she'll help with that." I shook my head, already thinking about the different people in the neighborhood who had mentioned places opening up.

"I'll help you find a place."

She tightened her arms around me, and I could've wept from happiness. "We have a lot to figure out. I want to hear about your plans too."

I smiled at her and pulled her farther into the store. "I'm excited to think about them with you." I stopped mid-step when I realized I hadn't asked an important detail. "Can you stay for Nochebuena?"

The signature mischievous Kiskeya smile came out, then: "I've already got an invite from your mom."

"My mom?" I balked. "Did she know you were coming?"

She tugged on my hand and brought me in for another kiss. Her tongue was like a drug and by the time I came up for air, I had no clue what we were even talking about. "I had a little help getting here."

It was like I'd been lit from the inside. "I'm so happy you're here, Kiskeya. I'm so glad you came."

"I'm exactly where I'm supposed to be. Merry Christmas, Sully."

I pressed my cheek to hers and held on tight. "Feliz Navidad, mi amor."

EPILOGUE

KISKEYA

One year and one day later

"Mmmm, Christmas morning has never been this good...keep going, baby."

I licked into Sully, the tip of my tongue circling her clit as she thrust her hips, pressing her pussy to my mouth. A year later and still I felt like I would never get enough.

"Come here, sweetheart." She beckoned, and immediately I lifted off and made my way up her body, looking for her mouth.

She was still wearing her pajama shirt, pushed up so she could play with her tits while I went down on her. I pinched one as I kissed her, open mouthed and hungry. I thrust my hips so she could feel the lubed dildo I'd strapped on before I got derailed.

"Si, damelo." She grabbed my ass and pressed me to her. Well aware nothing revved me up more than seeing her needy. "I gotta have it."

I brought my hand back down and dipped my thumb into her slick heat. "You're so wet for me."

"Always. Come on, babe." She moaned and I couldn't wait another second. I palmed the dildo and entered her slowly, her moans the only sound in our little studio apartment.

"Tell me how it feels," I gasped as I thrust in earnest, one hand leaning on the bed and the other rubbing circles on her clit.

"So good. Harder," she pleaded, as she rocked her hips with mine. "I'm so close."

I thrust in and out of her with the strap-on and worked my fingers on her exactly like I knew she liked. Soon, her legs were trembling with the incoming orgasm. She stiffened, her head thrown back, mouth open in a silent cry, as I fucked her through one, and then a second orgasm.

I pulled out and quickly took the strap off, knowing what she'd ask for next. As soon as she heard the thump of the silicone toy hitting the floor, she crooked her finger, eyes still closed.

"I'm sorry," I said, already crawling up her body. "I'm not sure what that means." I pressed myself to her, so she could feel how wet I was.

She opened one eye as she shoved a pillow under her head. "It means, *sit on my face.*"

Maybe someday, sex with Sully wouldn't be all-consuming. Maybe...eventually. But today, this room, this bed, this woman, it was my whole world.

"Come here, baby." I came to her as I always did, needing her, and immediately she licked into me. Strong hands gripping me tight, bringing my pussy to her mouth so she could have me, just like she wanted me.

"Mmm, yeah suck on that. Tighter, corazon." I leaned on the wall and rocked my hips as she kissed, sucked, and licked me into a frenzy. And soon I was coming, again, and again. When I was spent, I lowered my sated body until I was on my side face to face with the woman I loved.

"Merry Christmas, mi amor." It was useless to try and keep the smile from my lips.

"Feliz Navidad, mi vida." She said, tangling our feet together as she reached out for my hand, as if her calling me "her life" was no big deal.

"How about a summer wedding?" she asked as she looked at the engagement ring I'd put on her finger last night at her mother's house.

"I'd do it tomorrow. I just want to be married to you."

A sweet smile and more kisses were her answer. "Now that your job at the bakery will have more responsibility, it's probably better to wait a few months."

I shrugged at that. Canela, had just opened a new branch in the Upper West Side which I was the executive chef for. It was a great job, and I wanted to do well, but Sully, us, that was my priority. "I already let them know I may need time off for the wedding."

"So you've been this planning for a while?"

I scoffed and pulled her in for another kiss. "As if you didn't know that already."

"True, you're a chronic planner. We can think about timing later. I have the new bakers, and Mom is managing the finance side, so in theory, I can take time off." I grinned at how off-put she looked, even though her business was booming. Sully's online bakery had taken off this year. She'd started a nonprofit in the end, and part of the mission was to train survivors of domestic violence to bake commercially. A way for them to be financially independent. Her first couple of students had ended up doing so well, she hired them full-time. It was a beautiful project and I was so proud of her.

"We'll figure it out. I just want to honeymoon somewhere warm where I can have access to your body twenty-four-seven." It really was my only requirement.

"That can be arranged, I'm sure." She answered happily as I moved in to kiss her, already feeling the lust building again. I tangled my tongue with hers, my hands roaming over my favorite spots.

"Again," she encouraged as I opened her with my fingers, always ready for more.

Buzz. Buzz. Buzz.

"Leave it, babe. Don't stop." I wasn't planning to.

She was delivering fevered open-mouthed kisses as I touched her, when the phone on my side of the bed started buzzing too.

"Dammit." We both pulled apart as I felt around for the phone.

"You know it's my mother," Sully grumbled as she buttoned her pajama shirt.

I squinted at the screen and grinned. "It's your mom *and* my sister. She wants to Facetime later."

"I love that she likes me, but your sister's timing is as bad as my mother's."

I snorted as I sent texts to our family, assuring them we would surface eventually.

"I don't know what the rush is," my fiancée complained. "All Mami has this morning are leftovers and Mimosas."

"I got the mango custard pie. I didn't bring it last night because she told me if I left it there, she'd eat it," I said, still texting with Sully's mom.

She sucked her teeth, but I could hear the smile in her voice clearly. "You two and your weird arrangements."

"Magalys and I understand each other."

"Yeah, baby, you do." She leaned in and gently took the phone out of my hand. "No more texting. We'll be there soon. But let's enjoy our little nest before we have to go out into the snow. No rushing," she said, pressing a soft kiss to my mouth. "Today's a no-bake day, just a play day."

I smiled at that. "I love our play days. Te amo."

"Kiskeya, mi bella."

Our phones buzzed at the same time, probably a message from my sister or more instructions from her mother. But we ignored them all and took refuge under our warm blankets as the snow fell outside on our little corner of the world.

The End

ABOUT THE AUTHOR

Adriana was born and raised in the Caribbean, but for the last 15 years has let her job (and her spouse) take her all over the world. She loves writing stories about people who look and sound like her people, getting unapologetic happy endings.

When she's not dreaming up love stories, planning logistically complex vacations with her family or hunting for discount Broadway tickets, she's a social worker in New York City, working with survivors of domestic and sexual violence.

Her debut novel, *American Dreamer*, has been featured on Entertainment Weekly, NPR and was one of the TODAY Show on NBC's Hot Beach Reads picks. Adriana is an outspoken advocate for diversity in romance and has written for Remezcla and Bustle about Own Voices in the genre. She's one of the co-creators of the Queer Romance PoC Collective and is the President-Elect for the Romance Writers of America New York City Chapter.

Find Adriana:

Website: adrianaherreraromance.com

Thank you for reading. If you enjoyed this story, reviews are very welcome.

facebook.com/Adriana-Herrera-228231090202024460

twitter.com/ladrianaherrera

instagram.com/ladriana_herrera

ALSO BY ADRIANA HERRERA

American Dreamer

American Fairytale

American Love Story

American Sweethearts (March 2020)

Don't miss my next release!

Sign up for my newsletter for updates at
ADRIANAHERRERAROMANCE.COM

American Dreamer

A *TODAY* SHOW BEST NEW BOOK TO READ THIS SUMMER

No one ever said big dreams come easy

For Nesto Vasquez, moving his Afro-Caribbean food truck from New York City to the wilds of Upstate New York is a huge gamble. If it works? He'll be a big fish in a little pond. If it doesn't? He'll have to give up the hustle and return to the day job he hates. He's got six months to make it happen—the last thing he needs is a distraction.

Jude Fuller is proud of the life he's built on the banks of Cayuga Lake. He has a job he loves and good friends. It's safe. It's quiet. And it's damn lonely. Until he tries Ithaca's most-talked-about new lunch spot and works up the courage to flirt with the handsome owner. Soon he can't get enough —of Nesto's food or of Nesto. For the first time in his life, Jude can finally taste the kind of happiness that's always been just out of reach.

An opportunity too good to pass up could mean a way to stay together and an incredible future for them both...if Nesto can remember happiness isn't always measured by business success. And if Jude can overcome his past and trust his man will never let him down.

American Fairytale

FAIRY-TALE ENDINGS DON'T JUST HAPPEN; THEY HAVE TO BE FOUGHT FOR.

New York City social worker Camilo Santiago Briggs grew up surrounded by survivors who taught him to never rely on anything you didn't earn yourself. He's always dreamed of his own happily-ever-after, but he lives in the real world. Men who seem too good to be true...usually are. And Milo never ever mixes business with pleasure...until the mysterious man he had an unforgettable hookup with turns out to be the wealthy donor behind his agency's new, next-level funding.

Thomas Hughes built a billion-dollar business from nothing: he knows what he wants and isn't shy about going after it. When the enthralling stranger who blew his mind at a black-tie gala reappears, Tom's more than ready to be his Prince Charming. Showering Milo with the very best of everything is how Tom shows his affection.

Trouble is, Milo's not interested in any of it. The only thing Milo wants is Tom.

Fairy-tale endings take work as well as love. For Milo, that means learning to let someone take care of him, for a change. And for Tom, it's figuring out that real love is the one thing you can't buy.

American Love Story

No one should have to choose between love and justice.

Haitian-born professor and activist Patrice Denis is not here for anything that will veer him off the path he's worked so hard for. One particularly dangerous distraction: Easton Archer, the assistant district attorney who last summer gave Patrice some of the most intense nights of his life, and still makes him all but forget they're from two completely different worlds.

All-around golden boy Easton forged his own path to success, choosing public service over the comforts of his family's wealth. With local law enforcement unfairly targeting young men of color, and his career—and conscience—on the line, now is hardly the time to be thirsting after Patrice again. Even if their nights together have turned into so much more.

For the first time, Patrice is tempted to open up and embrace the happiness he's always denied himself. But as tensions between the community and the sheriff's office grow by the day, Easton's personal and professional lives collide. And when the issue at hand hits closer to home than either could imagine, they'll have to work to forge a path forward...together.

American Sweethearts

JUAN PABLO CAMPOS doesn't do regrets. He's living the dream as a physical therapist for his beloved New York Yankees. He has the best friends and family in the world and simply no time to dwell on what could've been.

Except when it comes to Priscilla, the childhood friend he's loved for what seems like forever.

New York City police detective Priscilla Gutierrez has never been afraid to go after what she wants. Second-guessing herself isn't a thing she does. But lately, the once-clear vision she had for herself—her career, her relationships, her life—is no longer what she wants.

What she especially doesn't want is to be stuck on a private jet to the Dominican Republic with JuanPa, the one person who knows her better than anyone else.

By the end of a single week in paradise, the love/hate thing JuanPa and Pris have been doing for sixteen years has risen to epic proportions. No one can argue their connection is still there. And they can both finally admit—if only to themselves—they've always been a perfect match. The future they dreamed of together is still within reach...if they can just accept each other as they are.

COMING MARCH 2020 - AVAILABLE FOR PREORDER

ALSO BY ADRIANA HERRERA

American Dreamer

American Fairytale

American Love Story

American Sweethearts (March 2020)

DON'T MISS MY NEXT RELEASE!

Sign up for my newsletter for updates.

ADRIANAHERRERAROMANCE.COM

Made in the USA
Middletown, DE
02 July 2024

56698892R00090